"Was it the FBI's intention all along to use me as some sort of bait?"

He hesitated a moment. "I don't know. They didn't think this guy would target you. In any case it doesn't matter."

She looked at him in disbelief. "Doesn't matter? That's easy for you to say," she exclaimed.

"It doesn't matter because nothing is going to happen to you," he said firmly. "I quit my surveillance job."

She gasped and moved out of his arms. "Does that mean you're going to leave here?" She was stunned by how much she didn't want to tell him goodbye.

"It means the exact opposite," he replied. "I'm not only going to stay here, but until these men are in jail or the danger has somehow passed, you've just earned yourself a twenty-four-hour-a-day bodyguard."

D0180111

CARLA CASSIDY

WANTED: BODYGUARD

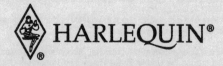

HARLEQUIN®

TORONTO • NEW YORK • LONDON
AMSTERDAM • PARIS • SYDNEY • HAMBURG
STOCKHOLM • ATHENS • TOKYO • MILAN • MADRID
PRAGUE • WARSAW • BUDAPEST • AUCKLAND

Recycling programs
for this product may
not exist in your area.

ISBN-13: 978-0-373-69488-4

WANTED: BODYGUARD

Copyright © 2010 by Carla Bracale

Printed in U.S.A.

ABOUT THE AUTHOR

Carla Cassidy is an award-winning author who has written more than fifty novels for Harlequin Books. In 1995, she won Best Silhouette Romance from *RT Book Reviews* for *Anything for Danny*. In 1998, she also won a Career Achievement Award for Best Innovative Series from *RT Book Reviews*.

Carla believes the only thing better than curling up with a good book to read is sitting down at the computer with a good story to write. She's looking forward to writing many more books and bringing hours of pleasure to readers.

Books by Carla Cassidy

HARLEQUIN INTRIGUE
1077—THE SHERIFF'S SECRETARY
1114—PROFILE DURANGO
1134—INTERROGATING THE BRIDE†
1140—HEIRESS RECON†
1146—PREGNESIA†
1175—SCENE OF THE CRIME: BRIDGEWATER, TEXAS
1199—ENIGMA
1221—WANTED: BODYGUARD

†The Recovery Men

Don't miss any of our special offers. Write to us at the following address for information on our newest releases.

Harlequin Reader Service
U.S.: 3010 Walden Ave., P.O. Box 1325, Buffalo, NY 14269
Canadian: P.O. Box 609, Fort Erie, Ont. L2A 5X3

CAST OF CHARACTERS

Lana Tyler—Her ordinary life as a widowed mother and jewelry designer exploded the day the FBI invaded her home.

Riley Kincaid—Hot and sexy, as an FBI agent he wants to get the bad guy, but he gets more than he bargained for with Lana and her daughter.

Haley Tyler—Was it possible Lana's little girl was a motive for murder?

Greg Cary—Lana's next-door neighbor. Is he guilty of horrific crimes or had the FBI gotten it wrong?

Seth Black—A friend of Greg's…and a partner in murder?

Joe Tyler—Had the dead cop known more than he'd said before he was murdered?

Trent Clayton—Greg's friend. Was he working with Greg to murder young women?

Chapter One

Lana Tyler silently crept out of the small bedroom and breathed a sigh of relief. Getting almost four-year-old Haley down for a nap was always a bit of a challenge and today had been no different, but finally, after two stories, a backrub and a drink of juice, the little girl had fallen asleep.

Now if Lana were lucky she'd get a couple of hours to herself. As she walked through the living room she eyed the overstuffed hunter green sofa with a touch of longing.

A nap for mommy wasn't such a bad idea, but she had a big jewelry show coming up in two weeks, and the best time for her to work on her new pieces was when her daughter was either napping or tucked into bed for the night.

A knock on the front door halted her progress from the living room to the kitchen, and she backtracked to see who was at the door.

Two men stood on her porch, both clad in dark

suits and wearing matching somber expressions that led her to believe they were either there to save her soul or to serve a warrant. She hadn't broken any laws that she was aware of, and as far as she was concerned her soul was in pretty good shape.

"Yes? May I help you?" she asked through the screen door.

"Good afternoon, Mrs. Tyler. I'm FBI Agent Bill McDonald, and this is Agent Frank Morrel." He opened a badge holder and held it up so she could see his official identification. "May we come in and speak with you?"

FBI? For a moment a rush of hope filled her, hope that somehow they'd come to tell her the name of her husband's killer, that finally, after twenty long months, she would have some closure.

She looked carefully at the badges and assured herself they were real, then unlocked the screen door and opened it to allow the two agents into her home. "Is this about Joe? Have you finally caught the person who murdered him?"

"Sorry, Mrs. Tyler, this is about another matter," Agent McDonald replied.

She frowned. "Another matter?" She gestured them into the living room, where they both sat on the sofa. "If this isn't about Joe, then what's it about?"

"We need your help," Agent Morrel said.

"My help?" Lana sank into the chair facing the two men. What could the FBI possibly want with her?

She was just an ordinary single mother working hard to get by.

"We'd like to put an agent in your home for the next week or two. He'd be undercover, and we'd like him to pose as your new husband."

Lana stared at first one man and then the other. "Excuse me?" She must have misunderstood what he'd said. "Did you say husband?"

Bill McDonald nodded and leaned forward. "We understand that you're friendly with your neighbor Greg Cary."

Again a rivulet of surprise swept through Lana. "Yes, we're friendly," she agreed. "He's been a good neighbor over the years and a huge support since my husband was murdered. Why, is he in some kind of trouble?"

"I'm afraid we can't go into any specific details," Agent Morrel replied. "All we need from you is the okay to put an agent here in your home to do some surveillance work. We can assure you that there is absolutely no danger to you or your little girl. All we ask of you is that you go along with the charade of a marriage and don't tell anyone the truth. Not family, not friends. It's imperative that everyone believe Special Agent Riley Kincaid is your husband."

"Riley Kincaid?" She felt like a parrot, repeating random words as she tried to make sense of what exactly they wanted from her.

Morrel nodded and looked at his wristwatch. "He's

a good man and has been assigned to this particular piece of the operation. He should be here within the next fifteen minutes or so."

Lana felt as if things were spinning way out of control. "Fifteen minutes? You certainly aren't giving me any time to think about all this," she said with a touch of resentment.

"What's to think about?" Agent McDonald asked. "We need you and your house, and as the widow of a law-enforcement official, we know you'll want to help out, to do your civic duty."

What on earth was going on? What could Greg have done that would warrant FBI interest and an undercover operation? "Is there somebody I can call and speak to about all this?" she asked, reluctant to agree to anything before talking to somebody in authority, somebody not currently sitting on her sofa.

Morrel nodded. "You can call Associate Deputy Director Chris McCall at the Kansas City field office."

Lana got up out of her chair and grabbed the cordless phone. It took her only minutes to get the phone number for the Kansas City FBI field office from information, dial it and be connected to Chris McCall, who had obviously expected her call.

"Our man Special Agent Kincaid will be as unobtrusive as possible in your home, in your life," he assured her smoothly. "I understand that this is short notice, and we certainly appreciate your cooperation in allowing us to use your home for the next couple of weeks. Agents Morrel and McDonald will be your contacts should any problems arise."

He went on to praise her once again for her co-operation and willingness to step up and help. The way Lana saw it, she didn't seem to have much of a choice in the matter.

She hung up the phone and returned to her seat in the overstuffed beige chair, not thrilled by this crazy turn of events. She'd only recently gotten accustomed to not having a man in the house. She wasn't exactly excited to welcome in a stranger.

"Why does he have to pretend to be my husband?" she asked.

"Wouldn't all of your neighbors find it odd for you to suddenly have a man living here?" Agent Morrel asked. "How could you explain the presence of our man to Greg Cary? I doubt if he'd believe that Special Agent Kincaid was your brother."

"I'm not sure he'll believe that I have a new husband," she replied.

Agent McDonald held her gaze intently. "It's important that you make him believe." There was a sudden harshness in his tone and a darkness in his eyes that caused a ripple of apprehension to waltz up Lana's spine. Again she wondered what they thought Greg had done.

"We're putting a lot of manpower and resources into this operation. We just don't want things to get screwed up." Agent Morrel offered her a tight smile, but the friendly gesture didn't quite reach the winter gray of his eyes.

At that moment there was a loud knock on the door and then it whooshed open. "Honey, I'm home," a deep voice called from the foyer. Lana stiffened.

He stepped into the living room and it was as if he sucked all the oxygen right out of the room. Tall, with curly dark hair and a face that had the bone structure of a model, he wore a pair of jeans that hugged his slim hips and a white T-shirt that tugged across impossibly broad shoulders.

He was definitely hot and exuded bold male sexuality, and as his vivid green eyes met hers, then slowly slid down the length of her, she felt a blush heat her cheeks and had the irrational desire to kick them all out of her house and quickly lock the door behind them.

He approached where she sat and held out his hand. "Riley Kincaid, and you must be my lovely bride, Lana."

Lana didn't take his hand, but she did stand, not wanting him to hover over her. "I can tell you right now, Mr. Kincaid, I'm not real happy about this," she said with a cool tone.

"Please, call me Riley, or better yet, call me honey," he replied with a slow, sexy grin. "And I promise you this won't be too painful. In fact most women I know would love to be my bride, pretend or otherwise."

"Then I guess I'm not like most of the women you know," she replied stiffly.

Agent Morrel cleared his throat. "We'll just get out of here and let you two work out all the details," he said. "Again, we appreciate your help," he said to Lana as he and his partner headed for the front door.

It had all happened so fast. One minute she'd been a simple, average widowed mother of a young daughter and the next she was part of a covert FBI operation with a man too sexy for his shirt looking at her expectantly.

Special Agent Riley Kincaid wasn't thrilled about the way this particular operation was going down, but he was definitely eager to get Greg Cary and his accomplice behind bars.

He'd been worried that this mock marriage thing could be awkward. After all, Riley was a healthy male, and being cooped up with a hot woman for a couple of weeks could definitely prove tempting, but thankfully Lana Tyler wasn't his type at all.

She had that girl-next-door, fresh-scrubbed look that had never attracted him. He preferred his women a little exotic, a lot sexy and definitely without happily-ever-after shining from their eyes. Although he had to admit that Lana's blue eyes were rather pretty.

"So, what happens now?" she asked, obviously ill at ease.

"I go get my things from the car and then we sit down and figure out our cover story." He headed for the door and then paused and turned back to her. "Oh, and for future purposes, as my new wife you should know that I love a big breakfast in the morning, I take my coffee black, and I sure wouldn't turn down a nice shoulder and back massage at the end of a long day."

She narrowed her blue eyes into a steely gaze. "Then I guess it's important for you to know, as my new hubby, that I do as little cooking as possible, I drink hot tea, not coffee, and if you really think I'm going to offer you a massage at the end of the day, then you're not only the most unprofessional FBI agent I've ever met, but also completely delusional."

Riley nodded in amused satisfaction. Good, she wasn't a total pushover. Beneath that long sandy-blond hair and those charming freckles that danced across the bridge of her nose was a touch of sass and a strong will. It was probably going to take both to get through this ordeal.

As Riley left the house and headed to his car in the driveway, he glanced next door where Greg Cary lived. These homes were small ranch houses, with little yard between them.

By setting up a camera with a telescopic lens in Lana's spare bedroom he would be able to see not only who came and went from Greg's home but also see into the man's living room. He was their initial target, but they suspected he had an accomplice and that's who they wanted to identify. Hopefully, within a couple of weeks they could get them both under arrest.

Greg Cary's house was painted white with traditional black shutters and a row of summer flowers lining the walkway that led to his front porch. It looked neat and respectable.

Nobody ever wanted to believe that the guy next door was a criminal. Whenever it was on the news that one of these creeps had been arrested, there were always interviews of stunned neighbors exclaiming that they never would have guessed that the quiet man next door was a maniac.

He fought against a small wave of irritation. This wasn't what he wanted to be doing. He was too impatient to be stuck on surveillance, but as he lifted the two suitcases from the trunk of the car he felt the painful twinge in his shoulder that had kept him on light duty for the last three months.

Nothing like a bullet to the shoulder to slow you down, he thought. He supposed he was lucky not to be on desk duty. He supposed he was lucky to be alive.

He definitely wasn't looking forward to sharing his personal space with a woman. As far as he was concerned women were good for a few hours, maybe a night of pleasure, but before dawn broke he wanted them out of his bed and out of his life.

As he reached Lana's porch he shot one more glance next door. Nothing stirred and nobody was in sight. By the end of the day he wouldn't be the only person keeping an eye on Greg Cary. There were at least half a dozen agents ready to rotate shifts to make sure that Cary didn't burp without somebody knowing about it.

Lana stood in the living room, her arms crossed and her features unreadable. "I don't really understand why you're here or exactly what it is you need."

"The first thing I need is your guest bedroom. Why don't I get unpacked and settled in and then we can talk about how this is all going to go down."

At that moment Lana's daughter cried out from down the hall. "Mama! I'm up!"

"You go take care of the kid. I'll unpack and we'll meet in the kitchen in half an hour or so," he said.

He followed her down the hallway and couldn't help but notice that her butt looked damn good in the tight jeans she wore. Her sleeveless pale-blue blouse exposed slender arms that held the faint blush of a summer tan. Most of the women he dated had that fake-bake tan, but Lana's looked all-natural.

She stopped at the first doorway on the left. "This is Haley's room. The guest room is that one." She pointed to the second doorway on the right, then disappeared into Haley's room and closed the door behind her.

She definitely was more than a little bit uptight, he thought. He sighed. That would only make his job here more intolerable.

He carried his suitcases into the guest bedroom, a small room with uninspired navy bedding and a generic landscape painting on the wall. It would do for as long as he was here.

The first thing he did was store his gun in the top dresser drawer, where it was out of the reach of a toddler who might get curious.

Then he focused on getting the two cameras set up and pointed in the right direction. They were high-tech stuff, infrared for night shots and with an option that would signal an alert if any movement was detected and he wasn't standing right there.

He angled one toward the front of the house, where it would capture shots of anyone approaching Cary's front door, and then focused the other toward the living room window.

At the moment there was nothing to see, no movement of any kind, nothing to indicate that anyone was in the room. But he knew Greg was home and probably plotting his next move.

A flash of an ancient memory exploded in Riley's head. The scent of baking cookies, a familiar body crumpled on the kitchen floor and blood everywhere.

His chest tightened at the memory and for a moment he felt as if he couldn't draw enough oxygen. Breathe. Breathe, dammit, a voice whispered in the back of his brain.

It wasn't until he consciously willed the vision away that he could draw air into his lungs again.

He didn't store the clothes he'd brought with him in the dresser drawers or the closet. He'd live out of his suitcase for the next week or two. Hopefully, this particular assignment wouldn't go on any longer than that.

With his equipment all in place, he left the bedroom and headed for the kitchen, where he could hear the sounds of Lana talking with her little girl.

As he entered the kitchen he instantly spied the toddler in her booster seat at the table, a streak of strawberry jelly across one plump cheek and a tumble of blond curls on top of her head. Even though Riley wasn't into kids, this one was definitely a little doll.

"Hi, kid," he said.

She smiled at him. "Hi, Daddy!"

"Her name is Haley," Lana said. "Haley, this man is Riley. Can you say Riley?"

Haley nodded. "Daddy," she repeated, and clapped her hands together in happiness.

Lana leaned with one hip against the counter. "I don't know why she's doing that," she said, obviously irritated.

"Do I look like your husband did?" he asked.

Lana shook her head. "Not at all. Joe was blond, and he was a smaller man than you are."

"Her calling me daddy works well with the little make-believe world we have to build quickly." He sat down at the table. "Is that coffee I smell?"

She nodded, her shoulder-length hair shining in the sunlight that streaked through the windows. "I decided to brew a pot to show you that I intend to cooperate, but in return I want you to tell me everything that's going on and exactly why you're here."

She poured him a cup, then sat at the table opposite him. He took a moment to study her features. She had a cute upturned nose and full Cupid-bow lips that looked as if they were just begging for a kiss. He frowned, irritated by his own wayward thoughts.

"Basically, I'll be staying in your guest room, although I've got extra backup at night so I can catch a couple hours of sleep. During the day I'll be manning a camera and watching what goes on next door at the Cary house, taking down license plate numbers and trying to identify anyone who comes to visit him.

Everyone you know, especially Greg Cary, has to believe that I'm your new husband."

"That's the part I'm having trouble with," she said. "How am I supposed to explain the sudden appearance of a husband in my life?"

He took a sip of the coffee, then explained. "We've got a cover story already in place. You and I met online about six months ago, one of those dot-com dating services, and of course the minute you saw my photo it was love at first sight."

She laughed and it lit up her face, making her look prettier than she had moments before. "Full of yourself, aren't you?"

"Maybe just a little," he replied agreeably. "Anyway, we met online. I'm from Arizona, and we talked on the phone and e-mailed each other for the last six months. We got together twice, once in Santa Fe and another time in Denver. The FBI knows that over the last six months you've traveled to jewelry shows in both those cities. We realized how much in love we were, and so last weekend we tied the knot in Vegas."

"Because you know I was at a jewelry show in Vegas last weekend." Her smile fell away and her eyes grew guarded. "What else do you know about me?"

"Lana Tyler, twenty-nine years old. Widow of Joe Tyler, fallen police officer shot at a convenience store while buying a gallon of milk. Your daughter was a cesarean birth, and since your husband's death you've been trying to build a line of jewelry that expresses your love of nature. You like to take your daughter for walks in the park and to feed the ducks, and you sometimes still sleep in one of your husband's old shirts."

He'd guessed at the last part but realized he'd hit the nail on the head when she gasped and shook her head, obviously appalled by how much they knew about her, about her life.

He could almost feel sorry for her, the way they'd barged into her life with no warning. But as far as he was concerned, the end justified the means.

"Lana, we checked you out thoroughly before deciding to use you. We had to know that we could trust you, that you were smart enough to be able to pull off a fake marriage with me so I could get close to your neighbor."

"But why? What do you think Greg is guilty of?"

He realized her eyes weren't an ordinary shade of blue, but rather with a touch of purple like a periwinkle. He held her gaze for a long moment, trying to decide if he should tell her the truth or not.

As the wife of a cop she would have had to be strong to cope with the stresses of her husband's work. As the wife of a murdered cop she had to use that core of strength to deal with her grief and still function as a single parent.

Lana Tyler was stronger than she looked, and he had a feeling she could take the truth, would demand it before truly offering her full cooperation.

"We believe Greg Cary has killed four women in the last four months and that within the next ten days he'll claim his fifth victim," Riley said. "Your neighbor, Lana, is a serial killer."

Chapter Two

Lana stared at him as if he'd suddenly begun to speak Martian. "Is this some kind of a joke? Am I being punked?"

He wrapped his long fingers around his coffee cup and shook his head. "I wish it were a joke, but to the family of his victims it's damn-straight not funny."

"If you all believe that he's killed these women, then why isn't he already under arrest?" she asked, struggling to make sense of everything.

"Lack of any real evidence," he replied.

She stared at him in confusion. "I don't understand. If you don't have any evidence against him, what makes you think he committed the murders?"

"Right now our case against him is strictly circumstantial. He knew all the victims. They all worked out at the gym where he works. He fits our profile, but unfortunately he has a solid alibi for one of the murders, and that has complicated things."

"I read about this in the paper, along with a

warning that women should be careful about whom they work out with in the local gyms. But if you don't have anything but circumstantial evidence, maybe he isn't guilty after all," she replied, still unable to believe that the man who had helped her light her pilot light on her furnace when it had gone out last fall, the man who had fixed her garbage disposal when it had gone on the fritz, could possibly be a cold-blooded killer.

"He's guilty all right. We all know it, and it's just a matter of time before he's arrested. But we think he's working with a partner." Riley lifted his coffee cup to his lips, and when he lowered it, he cast her a brash grin. "Now let's talk about our honeymoon plans. I'm thinking maybe a beach setting. I love a girl in a bikini."

Lana didn't like him. He was cocky and arrogant and wasn't even trying to make this as painless as possible for her. She broke eye contact with him and instead looked at Haley, who was smearing the last of her peanut butter and jelly sandwich across her plate.

She got up from the table, grabbed a dishrag and quickly cleaned up the mess, then got a box of cookies out and gave her daughter one of the wafers.

Haley smiled and held it out to Riley. "Daddy, you want a cookie?"

"No, thanks, kid," he replied.

Lana threw the dishrag into the sink and then

turned to face him once again, her lips thinned with displeasure. "Haley, her name is Haley, not kid. Apparently you don't like children?"

He shrugged his broad shoulders. "Kids are okay. As long as they're other people's kids."

She really didn't like him. "Is it too early to ask for a divorce?"

He grinned. God, the man had the sexiest smile she'd ever seen. Despite her dislike of him, it created a wave of heat that swept over her and undulated in her stomach. "Ah, don't be like that. I promise I'll grow on you."

"Like fungus?" she retorted. "I don't like you, Agent Kincaid, but I realize it's important that I do my civic duty. I would appreciate it if you would get on with whatever you need to do and be as unobtrusive in my life as possible."

He eyed her with open amusement and got up from the table. "I just want to let you know that you'll miss me when I'm gone." With that he picked up his coffee cup and ambled out of her kitchen.

"Bye-bye, Daddy," Haley said. "See ya later."

"Not Daddy," Lana retorted a bit crossly. She returned to the table and wrapped her hands around her cup, trying to digest everything that had happened in the last thirty minutes.

Greg Cary a serial murderer? She couldn't wrap her mind around it. There had to be some sort of a mistake. He'd been her neighbor for the last six years.

He'd been a bowling buddy of her husband's, a man who participated in the neighborhood watch program. Everyone in the neighborhood liked and respected Greg.

Surely if he were a criminal Joe would have known. Her husband might have been many things, but he'd been a terrific cop.

Thoughts of Joe brought with them a sliver of residual grief. He'd been her childhood sweetheart, the only boy she'd dated through high school, the only man she'd ever been intimate with. When they had married she'd thought they'd be together forever. She'd never foreseen the rocky road ahead and his untimely death.

His life insurance policy had been enough to pay off the house and put a little nest egg away. For the last year Lana had managed to eke out a simple living with the sale of her handcrafted jewelry.

"Mommy, I want down." Haley raised her arms to get out of the booster seat.

So much for getting any work done today, she thought as she lifted Haley to the floor. The rest of the afternoon would consist of her chasing Haley and making sure she didn't get into Riley's way.

Thankfully, for the remainder of the afternoon Riley stayed in the guest bedroom with the door closed and Lana alternated playing with Haley and preparing the evening meal. She'd decided to do hamburgers out on the grill. That and a bag of chips was all Mr. Hot FBI Agent was going to get.

At six o'clock she took Haley to the backyard and sat her in the shaded sandbox where she loved to play, then cranked up the grill.

As she waited for it to get to the right temperature, her gaze drifted to the house next door. Was it possible that beneath Gary's affable, pleasant outward personality lay the dark soul of a killer?

Despite the warm July air, a chill snaked up her spine. How many times had she read about serial killers and how their neighbors were stunned and appalled to discover that the good old boy next door was actually a crazed murderer?

She supposed there was no danger as long as Gary didn't suspect the truth—that she was cooperating with the FBI to bring him down. Even though she didn't like it, she understood how important the pretend marriage was in this scenario.

Gary would never have believed that she'd allow a boyfriend to move in with her and Haley. She had been quite vocal about the fact that she wasn't going to be one of those single mothers who paraded men through their daughters' lives. Although she realized she was close to being ready to entertain the thought of dating, of maybe finding somebody who would be special in their lives.

Gary also knew she didn't have any brothers or male family members. He knew that other than a sister who was often out of the country, she was pretty much alone in the world, except for Haley.

Her parents had been wonderful people who had loved travel and adventure. Unfortunately, four years ago they had decided to take a sightseeing helicopter ride over one of the Hawaiian volcanoes, and engine trouble had resulted in a tragic wreck. Both her parents and the pilot had perished.

Her older sister, Rachel, had married a very wealthy man who loved to travel and had homes in France and on the Mediterranean, and the two of them spent most of their time overseas.

As much as she hated to admit it, the mock marriage was the only way she could explain Riley's presence in her home.

As Haley played in the sand, Lana put the patties on the grill and closed the lid, then sat at the umbrella table on the patio.

Maybe this wouldn't be so bad, she thought. Surely he would spend all his time with his camera at the window in the guest room, and at night he would have to sleep. Maybe she wouldn't really have to interact with him much at all while he was in her home.

As if to prove her thoughts wrong, he opened the sliding glass door and stepped out onto the patio. Instantly every muscle in her body tensed. He filled the immediate area with his energy and a simmering sexuality as he walked with a loose-hipped gait toward the table where she sat.

"Steaks?" he asked, and pointed to the smoking grill.

"Burgers," she replied.

He slid into the chair next to hers, and his gaze shot across the short green hedge that separated her lawn from Gary's.

"Shouldn't you be surveilling or making notes or something?" she asked, unable to keep her irritation out of her voice.

"I never miss a meal," he replied with an easy smile. "Besides, the camera is still running and will catch anything I need to see. We've got men in the area also watching his house. I can't stay at the camera 24/7. It's also important that I maintain the aura of a normal relationship with you."

He smelled good, like clean male mixed with an expensive cologne. "What exactly is it that you're hoping to see?" She got up from the table and walked to the grill to flip the burgers and to get away from that provocative scent of him.

"Anything that looks suspicious. Anyone who comes to visit him."

She turned her back to face the grill and heard him release a deep grunt of surprise. She whirled back around to see a sandy, smiling Haley attempting to crawl up on his lap.

"Pick me up!" Haley demanded.

Riley looked at Lana and she thought she saw a moment of sheer panic on his face. It flashed for only an instant and then was replaced with that irritating cool amusement as he picked Haley up and deposited her on his lap.

She clapped her hands and squealed with happiness. "I told you I had a way with women," he said to Lana.

"She's too young to know any better," Lana retorted. She turned back to her burgers.

Oh, she knew his type all right. Handsome as sin and probably with little moral code, he would be accustomed to women making fools of themselves over him. He'd probably never heard the word *no* from any female. Well, he was in for a rude awakening if he thought she was just going to be another in a long line of conquests for him.

She smiled as she thought of the sand that was probably falling off Haley and into the cracks and crevices of Riley's jeans. Hopefully, some of that abrasive sand would end up in his briefs.

She was acutely aware of Riley's gaze on her as she took up the burgers. Haley had climbed back off his lap and returned to the sandbox, where she was digging with a plastic shovel.

"Come on, baby. It's time to eat," Lana said as she carried the burgers toward the back door.

"Thanks, sweetheart, I'm right behind you," Riley replied, as if she'd been talking to him. He got up from the chair and then bent down and swooped

Haley up in his arms. She squealed in delight as he carried her into the kitchen.

He plopped her into the booster seat and then sprawled in a chair at the table.

"There are cold sodas in the fridge," Lana said. "Why don't you grab a couple, and while you're at it get out the mustard and ketchup or whatever you might want on your hamburger." She wasn't about to allow him to just sit and be waited on.

While he rummaged in the fridge she wiped down Haley's hands and then put the burgers on buns and poured the chips into a serving bowl. She placed the food in the center of the table and sat down, then cut up a burger for Haley.

Riley joined her, and instantly she was inundated with sensory overload. His scent seemed to surround her, and she imagined she could feel the heat from his body reaching out to warm her.

Get a grip, she told herself. Granted, it had been a long time since she'd been around any man, but if the world held only Riley Kincaid she absolutely, positively wouldn't be interested.

"I love hamburgers," Haley exclaimed.

"Me, too," Riley agreed with an easy smile at the child. "And I love potato chips."

"Me, too," Haley exclaimed with a giggle, and popped a chip into her mouth.

He could even charm the girls that young, Lana

thought. Oh yes, she knew his type very well. All charm and no substance.

"I forgot something earlier," he said, and reached into his shirt pocket. He pulled out a lovely gold wedding band and laid it on the table in front of her. "I believe this is yours, Mrs. Kincaid."

She stared at the ring, oddly reluctant to pick it up and put it on. It had only been a month ago that she'd stopped wearing her wedding ring from Joe. That ring had come to represent heartache each time she'd looked at it.

It's just pretend, she reminded herself as she finally picked up the ring and slid it on her finger. It felt cold and alien against her skin.

"I think we should plan a little celebration," he said.

She looked at him warily. "What kind of a celebration?"

"A gathering to announce our marriage to your neighbors and friends." He grabbed a handful of chips and smiled at her, seemingly unconcerned that what he was asking of her was to invite a potential serial killer over for cake and punch.

Riley stood and stretched with his arms overhead, wincing slightly as the muscles in his wounded shoulder groaned silently in protest.

It was almost nine. He'd been sitting at the cameras since he'd left the dinner table. Throughout the evening he hadn't seen anybody going in or out of the house next door, nor had the camera caught Greg performing any incriminating act.

Lana had agreed to set up something four nights from now, on Friday, to introduce Riley to her neighbors. He could tell she didn't like the idea, would have preferred not lying to her friends and neighbors, would prefer that Riley simply go away.

But Riley was eager to meet Greg Cary up close and personal. He had a nose for killers, and he wanted to look into Greg's eyes, get a reading on the man he believed was responsible for four women's deaths.

The house was quiet as he left the guest room. About an hour earlier he'd heard Lana putting Haley to bed. As Lana had read the little girl a bedtime story, Riley had closed his eyes and listened to her voice.

She had a nice voice, low and with just a touch of something sexy. She amused him. His easy charm held no power over her. She appeared determined to dislike him, and that definitely intrigued him.

He walked down the hallway toward the kitchen, where the light was still on, and found her seated at the table working on her jewelry. She didn't appear to notice his presence as she worked with a soldering iron.

He remained in the doorway, taking the opportunity to study her. She was pretty in an unassuming way. If she wore makeup it was subtle, not screaming like many of the women that he usually dated wore. She had a slamming figure, full breasts and a tiny waist and shapely hips that could definitely turn a man's head.

"Is there something you need, Agent Kincaid?" she asked, not taking her gaze off her work.

"The first thing I need is for you to call me Riley," he replied and walked over to the table. "Calling me Agent Kincaid could ruin this entire operation."

He sat in the chair across from her and looked at the items she had strewn across the top of the table. Pieces of metal and semiprecious stones battled for space with tiny tools, spools of wire and velvet boxes displaying finished products.

"You do nice work," he said as he looked at the necklaces and bracelets she'd completed.

She set the soldering iron down and finally looked at him. "Thanks. I enjoy it."

"What are you working on now?"

"A necklace that will be part of my winter collection."

He wanted to keep the conversation flowing, not only enjoying the sound of her voice but also the momentary respite from the tension. "What's the difference between a winter collection and a summer collection?"

She leaned back in her chair and tucked a strand of her hair behind her ear. "Mostly color. My summer collection is filled with bold, chunky, brightly colored jewelry, and the winter one has the more traditional colors. There's a big show here in town in two weeks and I want to make sure I have plenty of pieces to sell."

"You make a living at this?"

"I do okay, although I'm certainly not getting rich," she replied. "Most women can't resist a beautiful piece of jewelry at an affordable price. I'm steadily building up a clientele that's respectable. My goal over the next couple of years is to get my jewelry into some of the upscale stores not only here in town but around the country."

"You sell it on the Internet?"

She nodded. "Right now most of my sales come in through my Web page, Designs by Lana. Speaking of jobs, as my husband, what exactly is it that you do?" She unplugged the soldering iron and leaned back in her chair once again.

He liked that she had a directness to her gaze, that there was nothing flirtatious or simpering about her. "I'm an investment broker. I do most of my work at home."

"Where's all your furniture and personal belongings?"

It was apparent that she was thinking, working all the elements of their subterfuge around in her head. He couldn't help but admire the intelligence that shone from her eyes.

"Right now it's all in storage," he replied. "I

couldn't wait to get out here to be with my bride, so I stored everything and decided that once I got out here I'd figure out what to do with my stuff."

"Where exactly did we get married? We need details if we're going to make it sound real."

"You're right," he agreed. "We got married by Elvis at one of those little white chapels."

She shook her head vehemently. "No way. I'm not the type and all of my friends would find that odd. A little white chapel is fine, but Elvis, as much as I loved his music, is definitely out."

For the next few minutes they discussed their wedding, deciding the name of the preacher and making up those little details that would make their story ring true.

Twice he made her laugh with his silly suggestions, and he was stunned by how much he liked the sound of her laughter. It did amazing things to her face, lighting her eyes and making the freckles dance across the bridge of her nose.

"It must be tough being a single parent," he said when they'd sobered and felt as if they'd solidified their story.

She shrugged and began to pack her jewelry items into the drawers of a large tote on wheels. "Sometimes it's rough," she replied. "Being alone is the worst part, but I imagine you don't have to worry about that much." She cast him a sly, knowing gaze.

"When I want company, I can usually find it." It wasn't a boast; it was merely a statement of fact.

"Finding company is different than finding somebody to share things with," she countered.

"I gather from that statement that you don't intend to be alone forever, that you will probably eventually remarry?"

"I would be open to the possibility. There were a lot of things about being married that I loved." She glanced down at the table but not before he saw a whispered pain darken her blue eyes.

An uncharacteristic softness swept through him. He knew what it was like to grieve, to miss somebody so badly you almost lost the will to live. "You got a bad deal," he said gruffly.

She looked at him once again and this time there was a steely strength shining from her eyes. "I'm not the only woman in the world to lose a husband. Bad stuff happens and you just have to deal with it. What about you, Riley? Ever been married?"

"Nope, and I have no interest in getting married. Footloose and fancy-free, that's the way I like my life."

"Sounds lonely to me."

He grinned. "Trust me, I'm never lonely."

"It's a good thing this marriage is just pretend, otherwise I have a feeling we wouldn't last together a month."

"A two-week marriage, that I can probably handle," he replied.

"I wouldn't want you to strain yourself with anything more lasting." She got up from the table. "And now it's time for me to say good night. Fresh towels are in the bathroom closet along with anything else you might need."

He stood as well. "No good-night kiss from my bride?"

"In your dreams," she replied with a wry grin. "Good night, Riley."

He watched as she left the room and then he walked over to the kitchen window and peered outside to the house next door.

It was dark and silent, as if Greg had already turned in for the night. All the FBI agents had assured Lana that there was no danger to her, but Riley knew that no operation was without danger.

Certainly he couldn't foresee what Greg's reaction might be if he discovered Lana was working with them to put the man on death row, but he had a feeling it wouldn't be a positive thing.

He sighed and turned away from the window, his thoughts returning to the woman whose life he'd interrupted.

He'd been relieved to realize she had a sense of humor. That would certainly make things easier for both of them. And he was surprised to realize that he liked her.

Not that it mattered. Even though he was flirting with her, he wouldn't lose sight of the fact that he had a job to do here and that his time with her was strictly temporary.

Stifling a yawn, he turned out the kitchen lights and headed for the guest room. Haley's door was open and on impulse he stopped in her doorway and gazed at her.

He didn't want a wife and he certainly had never considered having a family, but he had to admit that Haley was one of the cutest kids he'd ever seen.

He left her doorway and glanced down the hall to Lana's door. He'd only guessed that she occasionally wore an old shirt of her dead husband's to bed. He'd heard somewhere about widows doing things like that. On the nights she didn't wear that to bed he guessed she was probably a nightshirt or pajama kind of woman.

He frowned, wondering what in the hell he was doing even speculating on what she wore to bed. He went into the guest room, and after checking the cameras to make sure everything was on autopilot, he shucked his clothes and got into bed.

His day had begun at the crack of dawn with a meeting in the field office to get this all set up. Now, even though it was just after ten, he was exhausted. He knew that part of it was because his body was still healing from the bullet that had slammed into his shoulder three months ago.

He'd grab a couple of hours of sleep, knowing that the agents in the neighborhood would cover Greg's house. He rubbed his aching shoulder as he tried to get comfortable in the unfamiliar bed.

Who knew that the creep he'd gone to interview would suddenly pull a gun and start firing? If it hadn't been for the quick thinking of Agent Morrel, Riley wouldn't be alive.

Fortunately, the near-death experience hadn't changed his views on life or love. He hadn't had a sudden epiphany that made him want to jump into a relationship or make babies to ensure the survival of his lineage.

He closed his eyes and almost immediately fell asleep and began to dream and in his dream, he was back in that place and time where the nightmare resided and horror called to him.

He watched himself enter the house and immediately smell something odd, something underneath the faint scent of baked cookies. The unusual smell caused his stomach muscles to knot. Bad. He knew something bad had happened. He called out to her, and when she didn't answer the anxiety inside him grew stronger.

Even when he saw the bloody handprint on the wall next to the kitchen it didn't make sense, and he had no warning of what he was about to experience.

He walked into the kitchen and the first thing that struck him was the blood. It was everywhere.

Splashed on the walls, streaked across the floor. His brain began to scream at that moment.

He found her on the other side of the kitchen island, sprawled on her back on the floor, her eyes staring unseeing and a knife protruding from her stomach. It was only then that the scream that had been trapped inside him released.

"Riley! Wake up!"

He jerked awake and winced against the hall light that spilled into the room.

Lana stood next to his bed. "You were having a nightmare."

He sat up as embarrassment washed over him. "Sorry."

"No need to be sorry. You just scared me. You were yelling."

He raked a hand through his hair and glanced at the clock. It was almost midnight. "Did I wake up Haley?"

"No. Thankfully, she sleeps like a log."

As his eyes adjusted to the light in the room, he got his first good look at her. A pleasant surprise coupled with a faint heat filled him as he saw that contrary to his initial speculation she didn't wear pajamas to bed but rather wore a sexy black silk nightgown that skimmed her lush curves.

She must have seen something in his eyes that made her uncomfortable, for she backed away from his bed and to the doorway. "Good night," she said, and then fled from his view.

A moment later the hall light went out. Knowing that sleep would be difficult to achieve immediately, he got out of bed and walked to the window. He checked the cameras to make sure everything was working properly and then stared out at the darkened house next door, but his thoughts weren't on Greg Cary. Rather, he was thinking about Lana in her hot black nightgown.

Contrary to the impression he had given her, he hadn't been with any woman for a long time. Before the shooting he'd been working long hours, and after the shooting he'd discovered that most of the women he knew weren't particularly interested in hanging out with an invalid.

His initial impression had been that Lana was more than a little bit uptight, but that sexy nightgown had made him think there might be something more to her.

He got back into bed and closed his eyes, willing away the vision of her. It would be the height of unprofessionalism for him to get involved in any way with her. More than that, it would be completely unfair to her.

She'd already told him that she wanted to remarry, and he would never let anyone close enough for him to want that kind of a relationship.

As he remembered the nightmare that had brought

her into his room, a knot fisted tight in his chest. He might welcome her into his bed if given the chance, but there was no way in hell he would ever welcome any woman into his heart.

Chapter Three

"Surprise!"

Lana stared in shock at the familiar woman who stood on her front porch. "Rachel. This is a surprise." Her heart dropped to her feet as she eyed the large suitcase that set next to her sister's feet.

The past two days had been difficult enough without her sister showing up unexpectedly on her doorstep. "Jason and I were on our way back from France and he was going directly to New York for a couple of business meetings, so I told him it was the perfect time for me to drop in and spend a couple of days with you. Oh!" Rachel's eyes widened at the same time that Lana felt Riley's presence behind her.

"Hi," he said. "I'm the new husband, Riley."

Rachel's blue eyes widened even farther as she looked from Riley to Lana. "Uh, I'm the older sister, Rachel."

"Lana, why don't you take your sister into the

kitchen to do a little catch-up and I'll take her suit-case into the guest room," Riley said smoothly.

Lana stared at her sister, then back at Riley, her mind struggling to figure out how this was all going to work.

"Yes, Lana, let's go into the kitchen. It appears we have a lot to catch up on." Rachel linked her arm with Lana's and pulled her toward the kitchen while Riley stepped out to grab the suitcase and then disappeared down the hallway.

It wasn't until Lana had poured her sister a glass of iced tea and they both sat at the table that Rachel began with her questions.

"New husband? When did this happen? Where did you meet him? Why hadn't you mentioned him before, and where is my niece?"

"Haley is down for a nap," Lana replied, deciding to answer the easiest question first. She knew that this would be the first big test for her.

As much as she hated doing it, she had to convince her sister that her marriage to Riley was real. She'd figure out later how to smooth out all the lies she was about to tell.

In two days' time she would be introducing Riley to her neighbors at a backyard soiree she and Riley were throwing to announce her big news, but at the moment she had to get over this more personal hurdle.

As she told Rachel their official story she tried

not to worry about how this was all going to work. Having Rachel in the house over the next couple of days was definitely going to be a challenge.

When she was finished telling Rachel how she and Riley had met, where they'd gotten married and how happy she was, Rachel leaned back in the chair and eyed her curiously.

"There's no question he's one hot hunk of man, but this is so unlike you. It seems so impulsive. Internet dating? A Vegas wedding? That's so not your style."

"It was crazy and impulsive," Riley said from the doorway. "But getting married was also the right thing for us to do. We just couldn't wait any longer to start our lives together."

He deserved an Academy Award. The look he gave to Lana was so filled with love and with a simmering passion that if she didn't know any better she would have bought into it herself.

"Sit down, Riley, and let me get to know you better," Rachel said. "I need to assure myself that you're a good fit for my sister and my niece."

"He's a perfect fit," Lana replied, and smiled at Riley. He walked behind her chair and gave her shoulder a little squeeze, then sat down next to her.

For the next hour Rachel grilled Riley, asking what he did for a living, where his family was located and what his thoughts were on child rearing. She questioned him about his finances, his life goals, and Lana sat back and let him take the heat.

Riley handled the inquisition like a pro, and it didn't take long before Lana saw her sister's reservations melting away beneath Riley's charms.

He told Rachel that he was an investment broker, that he'd grown up in Arizona and that he was an only child. He smiled and indicated that he feared he would be a soft touch as a parent, that already Haley had him wrapped around her little finger.

Lana had no idea how much of what he said was true, but if she didn't know the real story she definitely would have believed everything he said. He was not only a sexy charmer but an amazing liar as well, she thought.

With each lie he told, Lana felt worse and wished she could just tell her sister the truth about the situation. It just felt so wrong to lie to Rachel.

By that time Haley was awake from her nap, and as Rachel played with her on the living room floor, Riley and Lana caught a minute alone in the kitchen.

"I moved all my things into your bedroom," he said in a hushed whisper. "And I also stored the camera equipment in the closet."

"What about your surveillance?" she asked worriedly.

"I've already contacted agents McDonald and Morrel, and we're going to just have to improvise until your sister leaves. They'll keep Greg's house covered until things settle back down here."

At that moment Rachel walked into the kitchen trailed by Haley. "Daddy!" Haley grinned at Riley and held her arms out for him to pick her up.

Although Rachel didn't seem to notice Riley's hesitation, Lana did. He took the little girl and immediately deposited her on his shoulders as she laughed in delight.

He might be a charmer, he might be hot as hell to look at, but he definitely didn't have the makings of a family man, Lana thought. Not that she wanted him to be her family man.

"Why don't I run out and grab a couple of pizzas for dinner?" Riley suggested as Lana motioned for him to put Haley back down.

"Please, don't go to any trouble on my account," Rachel protested.

"It's no trouble. I've got to pick up a few things anyway," Riley replied.

"And I'll make a big salad to go with the pizza," Lana said.

"I love pizza," Haley exclaimed.

"I think I'll go get settled in," Rachel said. "I'll be back in a few minutes to help you with that salad."

As Rachel left the room Lana felt some of the tension ease from her. Since the minute she'd opened the front door and seen Rachel on the stoop, nervous tension had stiffened her shoulders and twisted her stomach.

Lana placed Haley in her booster chair and gave her a couple of crackers to hold her until the pizza arrived. With both Rachel and Riley gone, she sank down in the chair next to Haley and smiled at her daughter. "What a tangled web we weave," she said softly.

"What?" Haley asked.

Lana smiled. "Never mind."

And this was just the beginning. On Friday night she would be deceiving all her neighbors and, more important, hopefully Greg Cary.

She got up from the chair and pulled from the refrigerator all the items she needed to make a salad. She was in the process of cutting up a green pepper when Rachel flew back into the kitchen.

Rachel walked over to her and grabbed her by the shoulders, her eyes wide. "There's all kinds of camera equipment in the closet. Please tell me that Riley isn't making tapes of, you know, the two of you together...like sex tapes."

Lana stared at her sister and then dissolved into laughter. "No!" she exclaimed. "Oh, no, it's nothing like that. Oh my God, Rachel, what are you thinking?"

"The worst." Rachel slumped into a chair. "I saw that stuff and suddenly had a vision of you and your new beau splashed across the Internet in all your naked glory."

Lana giggled again and then realized she needed to come up with a reasonable explanation for the camera equipment. "Actually, Riley is kind of an amateur videographer. He occasionally works weddings and things like that."

Rachel released a sigh of relief as Lana returned to chopping the pepper. "You hear about this stuff all the time, men talking women into making a sex tape and suddenly the tape is on one of those Internet sites for people to download."

"First of all, no man could ever talk me into doing something so stupid, and second of all, Riley isn't that kind of man," Lana said firmly.

"Aunt Rachel is funny," Haley exclaimed.

Rachel smiled and shook her head. "You're a lucky woman, Lana. I didn't think you'd ever find a man as handsome, as charming as Joe, but it looks like you've done just that. And Riley makes you happy?"

Lana moved from the pepper to a tomato. "Of course. If he didn't make me happy then he wouldn't be here with me." Once again she felt the burning desire to spill the truth to her sister. She could trust Rachel not to say anything to another soul. But even as she considered it, the agents' warnings went through her mind and she reluctantly dismissed the idea.

"I can't believe that in all our conversations you

never mentioned anything about him. You have always been good at keeping secrets."

"What are you talking about?" Lana asked.

"You didn't tell me you were pregnant with Haley until you were almost six months along. And now I find out you dated Riley and married him without even mentioning his name to me."

"I just wanted to make sure it was right before I told you about him," Lana replied.

The conversation turned to Rachel's latest travels, and by that time Riley had arrived with the pizzas and they all ate dinner.

After dinner Riley made coffee and they carried it into the living room and continued visiting. But with each passing moment Lana felt a tension building in her stomach as she anticipated bedtime.

She was going to have to sleep in the same bed with Riley. It was going to be awkward, but there was no way to avoid it. Rachel would definitely think it odd if Riley bunked out here on the sofa.

Lana put Haley to bed at eight, and after that each tick of the clock brought her closer to sleeping with a man she insisted she didn't much like, but who smelled so good and looked so hot.

It was ten o'clock when Rachel got up and said she was calling it a night. "Yeah, I'm ready to turn in, too," Riley said with a wicked grin at Lana. "I still feel like we're newlyweds."

"Isn't he cute," Rachel exclaimed.

"He's a real piece of work," Lana replied wryly.

As Rachel disappeared into her room and closed the door, Lana went into the bathroom and tried to figure out what made her more anxious, the thought that a serial killer lived next door or the idea of crawling into bed with Riley Kincaid.

She dressed for the night in a huge oversized T-shirt that hung on her curves and fell almost to her knees. She definitely wasn't going to wear one of the nightgowns that always made her feel sexy.

She went into the bedroom where Riley was seated on the foot of the bed, taking off his shoes and socks.

"I can't believe this is happening," she said softly as she moved to the left side of the bed where the alarm clock, a reading lamp and the paperback novel she was reading sat on the nightstand.

"Don't worry, I don't take up too much room," he said, and grinned. He stood and pulled his T-shirt over his head and she tried not to notice his splendid, muscled chest. What she did notice was the puckered skin and red angry scar on his right shoulder.

"What happened?"

"I got shot a little over three months ago," he replied. "That's why I got stuck on this surveillance duty. According to the doctors I'm not one hundred percent yet."

He looked a hundred percent to her. In fact he

looked far more than a hundred percent. "Is it true that your parents live in Arizona?" she asked.

"No. My dad left us when I was eight and my mother died when I was fifteen. I went into the foster-care system until I was eighteen."

"I'm sorry," she replied.

He shrugged. "It was a long time ago. You said it before. Bad stuff happens and you really have no choice but to get over it."

As his hands moved to the snap of his jeans, she quickly pulled down the sheets on the bed and crawled in.

She faced the wall and squeezed her eyes tightly closed, willing herself not to imagine what he looked like without all his clothes. But her mind exploded with an unwanted mental vision.

He turned off the overhead light, plunging the room into darkness. She felt the bed depress beneath his weight and every muscle in her body tightened. "You aren't naked, are you?" she asked.

"As a jaybird," he replied and then laughed. "Actually, although I usually sleep in the buff I am wearing a pair of briefs right now in deference to you."

"Could you maybe put on a snowsuit in deference to me?"

He laughed again, the sound a deep pleasant rumble. "Thank God you have a sense of humor, otherwise this whole mess would be intolerable."

It felt pretty intolerable to her right now. She could

feel the heat of his body, smelled that delicious scent of him, and a coil of warmth unfurled in the pit of her stomach. She recognized it for what it was—desire—and it stunned her.

She clung to the edge of the mattress and prayed that sleep would come quickly.

Riley awoke spooned around Lana's back, his arm slung across her slender waist. She was still asleep, and for several long, pleasant moments he didn't move. Her hair smelled like apples, and she was warm as toast against him.

It was odd for him to awaken with a woman in his arms. He rarely spent the night with anyone and he never let anyone spend the night with him. He preferred to avoid the awkward mornings after whenever possible.

Going to sleep had been equally awkward the night before. Lana had claimed the very edge of the bed and her tension had filled the room. He had been disappointed that she'd traded her sexy nightgown for an oversize nightshirt, although he'd noticed her shapely legs beneath the nightwear.

Eventually she'd fallen asleep, but he'd remained awake long into the night, wondering if this whole operation was doomed to failure.

The murder timeline indicated that Greg was due for another kill in the next week. They had a couple of agents working out at the gym where Greg worked, hoping to see if he paid special attention to anyone, had any of the women there in his sights.

For the last couple of days, though, Greg had seemed to be on his best behavior. He went to work and then came home and didn't leave his house again. There had been no visitors to his residence. They had tapped his landline but suspected he was using toss-away pre-paid cell phones for any conversations he might be having with his partner in crime.

Lana stirred but didn't awaken, and Riley rolled away from her. He knew if she did wake up and found herself cuddled intimately in his arms she would be appalled.

So far she'd been a pretty good sport about things. He didn't want to make it even more difficult for her. He slid from the bed, grabbed his jeans and pulled them on, then snapped on some clean clothes and headed for the bathroom.

As he stood beneath the hot spray of water he was surprised to realize that he liked Lana Tyler. She was uncomplicated and didn't hesitate to speak her mind. She was a refreshing change for him.

Before he'd fallen asleep last night he'd felt something else for Lana—a faint stir of desire. It had whispered through him and it had only been by sheer willpower alone that he'd tamped it down.

When he walked into the kitchen minutes later

he was surprised to see Rachel already dressed and seated at the table, her suitcase on the floor next to her.

"Good morning," he said, glad to see that she'd made a pot of coffee. "I hope you slept well."

"Like a baby," she replied. "I have a taxi coming to pick me up."

Riley eyed her in surprise. "Is something wrong? I thought you had planned to stay for a couple of days."

"I had, and no, nothing is wrong. I got a call from my husband this morning. His business meetings were canceled and he's made arrangements for us to travel to China. This morning I'm flying to New York to meet up with him."

Riley couldn't help the wave of relief that flooded him. He could set the cameras up and move back into the guest room. "Lana will be disappointed that you couldn't at least stay for our little celebration tomorrow night."

"I'm disappointed, too. But it's nice to know I'm leaving Lana and Haley in good hands." She smiled at Riley, and he felt a stab of guilt at the lies he'd told the woman.

He reminded himself again that the end justified the means and that the ultimate goal was to put away a dangerous man.

At that moment Lana came into the kitchen and

a horn sounded from outside. Hasty goodbyes were exchanged, and then Riley carried Rachel's suitcase out to the awaiting cab.

Lana stood in the doorway and waved at her sister, then Rachel grabbed Riley and hugged him. "Take care of them, Riley. They've already had so much heartbreak in their lives." She released him, then slid into the backseat of the taxi and waved as the driver pulled away.

As he walked back to the door Rachel's words thundered in his head. He didn't want to feel responsible for Lana and her daughter. He just wanted to get this job done and move on. Moving on was what he'd always done best.

"That's a relief," Lana said as he came back into the house. "I love my sister, but this wasn't the best time for a surprise visit."

"You did really well. I know it was difficult for you to lie to her." He moved closer to Lana. She looked so pretty clad in a pair of navy shorts and a white-and-navy tank top. Her hair sparkled with gold highlights, and he remembered how it had smelled faintly of apples.

"You are a consummate liar," she said with a smile. "So smooth and effortless."

"It's just part of the job," he replied.

"I'm sure it's a gift that has come in handy in your personal life, too."

He cocked his head and looked at her curiously. "Are you trying to pick a fight with me?"

A faint blush swept into her cheeks. "Of course not," she replied.

"I don't lie in my real life." He wasn't sure why, but it was suddenly important to him that she understood that. "It's much better to be honest and let people know where you're coming from."

He wanted to kiss her. The desire came out of nowhere and slammed into his stomach. Maybe it was because his senses were still filled with the way she'd felt in his arms or the way the clean, sweet scent of her had filled his head. Or maybe it was because she just looked so damned kissable.

"I enjoyed sleeping with you last night," he said as he took another step closer to her. "It was kind of nice how you wanted to cuddle."

Her eyes widened and her lower lip trembled slightly. "You're lying now."

He smiled. "Okay, we didn't cuddle."

"I think maybe you're the one who is trying to pick a fight," she said.

She was right. Maybe he was trying to make her mad so that he wouldn't want to taste her lips, so he could forget how soft and warm she'd been in his arms.

"I'm going to get my equipment set up again. It's

time to get back to work." He said the words more for his own benefit than for hers.

He wasn't here to flirt and kiss Lana Tyler. He was here to do a job. And he'd do well to remember that.

Chapter Four

The backyard was almost ready for the party, and Lana had never been so nervous in her entire life. There were three married couples coming from the neighborhood, people Lana and Joe had often socialized with before Joe's murder. And of course there was one suspected serial killer coming as well.

Haley was down for a late nap, and the house was silent except for the slightly rapid beat of Lana's heart.

As she put a cake on a platter she looked out the window where Riley was sweeping off the deck.

He'd been distant since Rachel had left. He'd spent most of the time in the guest room and had come out only to eat.

She told herself that was the way it was supposed to be, but a small part of her missed his ridiculous flirting and charming smile.

He would be at his charming best in an hour, when

the guests began to arrive. And it worried her more than just a little bit that she liked his charm.

"Been there, done that," she now muttered to herself, and a deep grief stabbed through her as she thought of her dead husband.

Even though she'd told Riley that she didn't intend to be alone for the rest of her life, a part of her simply wasn't ready for the dating scene, for inviting another man into her life. She wanted somebody special. She wanted a father figure for Haley and a man to fill her loneliness. But she intended to be picky. It would take a very special man to fulfill all her desires.

She tensed as he came in the back door.

"Nervous?" he asked.

"You have no idea," she replied, and was surprised to hear that her voice was slightly shaky.

He walked over to her and placed his hands on her shoulders, and his green eyes held a softness she'd never seen there before.

For just a moment she wanted to fall into those green depths. She tried never to think about the aching loneliness that sometimes gripped her since Joe's death, but now with Riley's hands on her shoulders she realized how hungry she'd been for a gentle, simple touch from a man who had softness in his eyes.

"You'll do just fine," he said. "I'll stay close to you all evening, and if you get into any trouble I'll be there to make it right. Don't worry. Just relax and enjoy the evening."

"I appreciate that," she replied. Maybe it was the anticipation of the night to come that had her feeling half breathless. Or maybe it was because Riley stood so close and his eyes were so green and he smelled like crisp, clean male and that wonderful, slightly spicy cologne.

His eyes deepened in hue, and she knew in that instant that he was going to kiss her, knew she should step away from him and halt it before it began. But she didn't. She remained frozen in place, waiting with an eagerness that was stunning.

His lips touched hers with a simmering fire that quickly spiraled out of control as she opened her mouth to him. Their tongues battled as his hands left her shoulders and instead wrapped around her waist, pulling her intimately against him.

She raised her arms to link about his neck, loving the taste of him, the desire she tasted in his kiss. It didn't matter that he was definitely not the kind of man she wanted in her life. It didn't make a difference that he was only here temporarily and then would be gone.

All she cared about was that for this moment he made her feel wonderfully alive and desirable, and she hadn't felt that way for a very long time.

He tasted of something hot and wild, of unspoken danger and sin, and she loved it.

"Mommy. Daddy. Stop kissing and talk to me."

Lana jumped back from Riley at the sound of Haley's voice. The toddler stood in the kitchen doorway, a smile of pride of her face. "I woked up and now I want to go to the party," she exclaimed.

"It's going to be a few minutes before the party starts," Lana replied. She walked over and scooped up the little girl in her arms, then looked at Riley. "We both know that was definitely a mistake," she said.

"Only if you think it was," he replied. He leaned against the counter. "It didn't feel like a mistake to me. As long as we both know the score, as long as you understand that as soon as we get what we need on Greg I'm out of here, then it wasn't a mistake. It was just a moment of pleasant connection."

"A mistake," she repeated.

He smiled. "As long as we don't make any mistakes tonight we'll be fine."

"Speaking of tonight, I need to go change my clothes and I need to dress this little pumpkin."

"I not a punkin," Haley announced.

Riley laughed and the tension between them eased. "You want me to keep an eye on her while you get dressed?"

Lana looked at him in surprise, touched by the offer. "Are you sure you wouldn't mind? It would definitely make things easier on me."

He held out his arms and a happy, giggling Haley

went to him. "Come on, kid, let's go find some toys." As he carried Haley down the hall to her bedroom, Lana went into her own bedroom to get ready for the evening to come.

How do you dress for a party where you're going to lie to all your friends? Lana wondered as she stood in front of her closet.

What was Riley's favorite color? She had a feeling he'd like his women to wear bold, sexy colors. She nearly slapped herself. What was she doing? It was that kiss. That crazy kiss that had warmed her to her toes.

Forget it, she told herself. She needed to focus all her thoughts, all her energy on getting through the night.

She did just that, and forty minutes later everything was ready for the guests to arrive. She watched Haley race around the living room with her usual energy.

"You're going to be just fine," Riley assured her, as if he sensed the tension that screamed inside her.

"I hope so."

"It's important that you treat Greg like you always do. If he senses something off in you he might get suspicious, and that's the last thing we want."

She nodded, but wondered how it was possible to treat a man like a well-liked neighbor when you knew he might be someone who killed women for sport or pleasure or whatever perverse need drove him.

She hadn't seen Greg since Riley had arrived at her house. They rarely saw each other during the week. It was usually on the weekends that they might visit with each other as they each worked in their yards.

She froze as the doorbell rang. "We're on," Riley said, and walked with her to the door to answer it.

She was relieved when the first guests were two of the couples that had been her friends for several years. They were delighted by the news that Lana had remarried. Riley took them outside and fixed them drinks while Lana and Haley remained inside for the last of the guests to arrive.

As the doorbell rang once again, Lana peeked out to see Greg standing on the porch. This was what it was all about. This was probably one of the most difficult things she would ever do.

She drew a deep breath and then opened the door with a smile. "Hey, neighbor," she said, hoping her smile didn't feel as forced as it felt.

"Lana, you look lovely as usual," Greg said as he stepped into the house.

Greg Cary was a nice-looking man with pleasant but ordinary features and light-brown hair that he kept neatly trimmed. His best assets were his wide smile and the warmth of his brown eyes.

"The invitation mentioned a celebration. What are we celebrating?" he asked curiously.

"My new husband," she replied, and then forced a

laugh at his look of stunned surprise. "I know, it all seems very sudden, but it's really not. We've known each other for six months."

Haley walked over to Greg and gave him a happy smile. "Uncle Greg, we're having a party!"

"So I've heard," he replied. As he bent down and lifted the little girl into his arms Lana fought the desire to yank her daughter away from him. But that would definitely be odd. Greg had always been very good with Haley.

"So, that means you have a new stepdaddy," he said to Haley and then looked back at Lana. "This is certainly a surprise. You know I want to hear all the details," he said.

"I'm just waiting for Helen and Bill to arrive. But if you want to meet the man of the hour, he's in the backyard," she said.

"I can't wait to meet him, although you know I'm a bit hurt that you didn't tell me about him before now."

Was there a new darkness in his eyes or was she just imagining it? "If it's any consolation, I didn't tell anyone, not even my sister," she replied.

Greg smiled. "I guess that makes me feel a little better. So, what kind of a man is he? What kind of a father is he going to be to this little pumpkin?"

"I not a punkin," Haley exclaimed.

"You know I'd never put her at risk with the wrong kind of man," Lana replied.

"I guess I'll head out back and check out this new man of yours," he said.

Lana breathed a sigh of relief as she took Haley back in her arms. As Greg headed for the backyard she fought against a horrible chill that threatened to consume her.

On the surface Greg Cary appeared to be a friendly man who was well liked by his neighbors. However, there were two things Riley noticed about the man that he found both intriguing and telling.

First, it was obvious despite the friendly handshake and small talk that Greg didn't like Riley. Second, Riley noticed that despite his friendliness with his neighbors, there was also something subtly guarded about the man.

What he'd like to do was befriend Greg, maybe get an invitation into his home. He knew that Lana's late husband, Joe, had been friendly with Greg.

Had Joe sensed something off in his neighbor? Was it possible he'd gotten close to Greg not because of friendship but rather because he'd suspected Greg of something?

Riley and his team suspected Greg of killing four women, but all of those murders had occurred after Joe had been shot in a convenience-store parking lot. Were there other murders that they hadn't yet tied to Greg? And if that was the case, was it possible Greg was responsible for Lana's husband's murder?

All these questions whirled around in his head as he got to know the neighbors better and listened to them tell him what a paragon of virtue Joe had been, what a terrific husband he'd been to Lana and how delighted they were that she'd found happiness again.

As much as everyone seemed to like Greg, it was obvious they all positively adored Lana and Haley. And Joe, in death, seemed to have become a bigger-than-life neighborhood hero whom everyone had loved.

Greg was the first to leave, at just after eight. One by one the couples left as well, until by nine o'clock it was just Lana and Riley and an exhausted Haley left.

"I'm going to put Haley to bed and then we can talk," she said as she picked the girl up in her arms.

Riley wasn't sure who looked more tired, the toddler or Lana. As they disappeared down the hallway, he reminded himself of just how stressful the night had to have been for Lana.

When this was all over he'd walk away. He wouldn't have to face the consequences of their lies with friends or neighbors. He wouldn't have to pick up the pieces of broken trust with the people he cared about.

He walked into the guest bedroom and checked the cameras, then stared across the yard to Greg's house. It looked as if the man had already gone to bed. The house was dark and nothing stirred.

He wasn't sure why, but he had a bad feeling about this. There was nothing specific he could put his finger on that had him unduly worried, but it was there nevertheless.

He left the bedroom and went into the kitchen. Playing pretend husband all evening had created a side effect he hadn't counted on, a crazy desire for the woman who was pretending to be his wife.

They'd done a lot of touching over the course of the evening, the kind of affectionate touching that newlyweds did. As he'd visited and joked with the neighbors he'd realized this was a part of married life he'd never thought about before—the sharing with neighbors, the comfortable feeling of looking across a table at the woman you loved. Not that he loved Lana. He hardly even knew her.

Seeing the dishes that had been stacked on the counter, he began to rinse them and put them in the dishwasher. He'd almost gotten them put away when Lana returned to the kitchen.

"You didn't have to do that," she said as she sank down into a chair at the table.

"You wouldn't have had the mess if I wasn't here," he replied. "There's still some coffee left. You want a cup?"

"No, thanks. Actually, I'll take another glass of wine."

Riley poured her a glass of red, then got himself a cup of coffee and joined her at the table.

"I think the evening was a success," he said. "I think he bought our story."

"Good. I hope it was worth my screaming, frazzled nerves," she replied with a rueful grin.

He reached across the table and covered one of her hands with his. "I know this is tough, Lana." He felt the small tremor in her hand and he squeezed it more tightly. "You did fantastic tonight." He reluctantly released her hand and she picked up her glass and took a sip.

"I want to know the details," she said.

"Details about what?"

"About the murders. The newspaper article I read was fairly vague. I want to know everything that you know."

He looked at her in surprise. "Why would you want to know about the details?"

A frown line raced across her forehead. "Because all evening whenever I looked at him, whenever I talked to him, my head filled with all kinds of horrible visions. I think knowing the truth would be easier than everything I've been imagining."

He wasn't sure he agreed with her but decided she had a right to know. For all intents and purposes she was an integral part of the team working to put Greg behind bars. "What exactly is it that you want to know?"

She took another sip of her wine. "How were they killed?"

"Beaten and stabbed multiple times."

Her eyes darkened. "Where were they killed?"

"In their homes. Two of the women were dressed in workout clothes, as if they were either getting ready to go to the gym or had perhaps set up an at-home session."

"And no forensic evidence was found? The killer didn't drop some DNA that you could use to catch him?"

"Unfortunately, nowadays that happens less and less. With all the crime shows on television we've educated our criminals very well. They're smarter, more careful than they used to be." And Greg Cary seemed to be smarter than most, he thought.

"Tell me about the victims."

He leaned forward. "Lana, why would you want to hear all this? Hearing about the victims won't help anything."

"It will help me," she protested. "Every time I feel weak doing this job, I want to have a name of a woman to think about, to give me strength to go on."

Riley certainly didn't have to reach for the names of the victims. He'd studied each of the case files with a need that bordered obsession. Every detail of the victims' lives and deaths were emblazoned in his brain.

"The first was Melinda Huff, a twenty-seven-year-old woman who was killed in her kitchen at approximately two in the afternoon. Her two-year-old daughter was in a crib in the bedroom, and her body was found by her husband of four months."

"He was checked out?" she asked.

Riley nodded and leaned back in his chair. "As always in these kinds of cases, the first person we look at is the husband. We couldn't find a motive, and friends and family members told us the marriage had been a happy one. But he remained our main suspect."

"Friends and family members don't always know what goes on behind closed doors," she said, and for a moment he thought her eyes darkened with secrets of her own.

"Exactly, but the second murder changed everything. The crime scene was the same. Debbie Warren had been beaten and stabbed and her body was found just inside her front door. Her children were at school and her husband had a solid alibi for the time of the crime. By the time the third murder occurred we knew we had a serial killer on our hands. The only point of intersection in all the women's lives was that they all worked out at Harry's Gym."

"Where Greg works," she said flatly. "But surely there are other men at the gym who could be responsible."

"Of course, and we've investigated all of them and

one by one discounted them all, except for Greg." Once again he leaned forward. "I've studied serial killers for the last ten plus years. Each and every victim kills a little piece of me. I know in my gut that Greg is responsible. He's a man who likes power, and working as a trainer in the gym gives him a sense of power. At heart he's a loner, but he's managed to keep up a front that is friendly, yet superficial."

"What makes you think he has a partner?" she asked.

"For two of the murders there were indications that two people were present. And for one of the four deaths Greg had an alibi. But we believe we have two men killing together when possible and separately to throw us off. We think Greg is the puppeteer, that he chooses the victims and has somebody killing for him. I really can't give you the details."

"But isn't that odd?" She tucked a strand of her hair behind her ear, a gesture he'd come to recognize as a nervous one.

"It's unusual, but not unheard of. Leopold and Loeb were two college students who wanted to commit the perfect crime. Angelo Buono and Kenneth Bianchi were cousins who became known as the Hillside Stranglers."

"Who do you believe might be Greg's partner?"

Riley shrugged. "We don't know for sure, although we suspect it might possibly be somebody he trains, somebody who is impressionable and can be easily manipulated."

"That's a terrible thought," she exclaimed.

"Tell me about your husband," he said, wanting to change the subject and take her mind off Greg and his victims. "From everything I heard from your neighbors tonight he was a terrific guy."

"Everybody loved Joe. He was the life of the party, the go-to guy if you needed help with anything." She picked up her glass and downed the last of her wine.

"How long were you married?"

"We got married when I was twenty-two, and we'd just celebrated our fifth anniversary when he was killed. But we were high school sweethearts and had known each other since grade school."

She got up from the table and carried her glass to the sink. "I'm exhausted. I think I'll call it a night."

"Yeah, me, too." He took his coffee cup and added it to her glass in the sink, then took her by the shoulders. "I know how tough this is on you, Lana. I'm sorry we're having to put you through all this."

Her eyes lightened slightly and a small smile curved her lips. "I think you're a nicer man than I initially thought you were, Riley Kincaid."

He laughed. "Thanks, I think." He sobered as he remembered the kiss they had shared. He wanted to kiss her again. Even though she wasn't his type, even though he was here to do a job and then would be gone, he couldn't deny that something about her stirred him on a physical level.

And he knew he affected her the same way. He could tell by the flare of her eyes, by the way she caught her breath and held it as he rubbed his hands on her shoulders.

"You know that mistake we made earlier today?" he asked.

She trembled slightly and her eyes deepened to a purple shade of twilight. "What about it?" There was a breathy quality to her words that torched a new burst of heat through him.

"I'm thinking about repeating it."

"Do you really think that's a good idea?"

He smiled at her, encouraged that she hadn't stepped away from him. "Right now I don't think I care whether it's a good idea or not."

Her tongue darted out and licked her lower lip. He knew it was an unconscious gesture, but it merely heightened the desire that now roared through him.

"So, what are you going to do about it?"

The words were barely out of her mouth before she had her answer. He took her mouth with the hunger that had been building inside him all evening and she responded with a hunger of her own.

Her mouth was hot and eager beneath his and excitement ripped through him as she wound her arms around his neck and pressed more closely against him.

He tangled his hands in her hair, loving the way the silky strands felt against his skin and the small moan that escaped her. He moved his mouth from hers and kissed across her jaw and down her throat.

She dropped her head back, allowing him better access to the sweet skin of her throat, and he slid his hands from her hair and down her back to her hips.

He didn't understand it, but he wanted this woman more than he could remember wanting a woman in a very long time, and he wasn't the kind of man who spent time analyzing his own wants and needs. He simply took what he wanted, what he desired.

Pulling her more tightly against him, he knew she could feel his arousal, and when she didn't try to step away from him, he also knew she wanted him as badly as he wanted her.

"I want to make love to you, Lana," he whispered, and pulled back slightly to watch her response. Her eyes were slightly glazed as she stared up at him.

At that moment a buzzing resounded from the guest bedroom. Riley instantly dropped his arms from around her as a different kind of adrenaline shot through his veins.

"What's that?" she asked.

"My camera," he replied. "It means somebody next door is on the move." He raced into the bedroom and grabbed his gun from the top drawer of the dresser, then headed out the front door, desire replaced by the determination to see what the killer next door might be doing.

Chapter Five

Lana stood in the center of the living room, a touch of fear battling with the residual desire that Riley had created in her.

She stared at the front door and wondered what was going on outside. Was Riley in danger? Was it possible that they hadn't fooled Greg after all?

Greg had been in the house alone once during the evening, when he'd come in to use her bathroom. Riley had carefully set the stage for just that occurrence. The cameras had been stored in the closet, his clothes had been hung in her closet, and she'd thought they'd covered all the bases.

Had they missed something?

She walked over to the sofa, sank down on the edge and drew a deep breath to steady the rapid beat of her heart. It was an accelerated pulse that had begun the moment Riley had started kissing her.

She understood now how widows sometimes made bad decisions in new relationships. When the loneliness got too great, when the need to be held or desired grew overwhelming, then they were vulnerable to falling into the arms of the first man who took any kind of an interest in them.

Even though she didn't want Greg to hurt any more women, even though she didn't want Riley to be in danger, she was grateful that the alarm had sounded. Otherwise she might have found herself in bed with Riley.

Just thinking about it created a rivulet of heat that swept languidly through her. Kissing Riley was a mistake, and making love to him would be the biggest mistake of all.

Even if he suddenly fell to his knees and proclaimed that he loved her, that he wanted to be a part of her life, part of Haley's life, he simply wasn't the kind of man she wanted. She wasn't sure what she wanted in the man she eventually invited to be a part of her life, but she knew exactly what she didn't want—and that was a man like Riley.

Besides, she could never be enough woman for a man like Riley. She shook her head to shove this thought away.

Where was he? What was going on outside? She rose from the sofa, too nervous to sit still another minute. There was a tiny part of her that wanted to believe that Riley and his FBI cohorts had gotten it wrong, that Greg was truly as he presented himself— a nice man with a good heart. Not a killer.

It was almost thirty minutes later when Riley finally returned to the house, his features etched with frustration. "I think maybe it was a cat or a raccoon that set off the alarm," he said. "None of the other people watching the house saw anyone go inside or leave, so I guess we can chalk this up to a false alarm."

"Thank God," she said. Once again she sat on the sofa. "Riley, we need to talk."

"About what?"

She looked at the wall just behind him, finding it impossible to look directly at him. "About this crazy sexual attraction we seem to share." She shot him a quick glance that caught his lips curving up in one of his hot, sexy smiles.

"What about it?" he asked and to her dismay he moved over to the sofa and sat next to her.

"I don't want it," she replied. She felt the heat of a blush warming her cheeks. "I'm not looking for a hook-up. In fact, all of this has made me realize that I'm not looking for anything right now. Tonight with all the neighbors, it all just brought back so many memories of Joe."

The smile on his face fell away and his eyes filled with that softness that drew her in, that made her want to fall into his strong arms and have him hold her through the long, lonely night.

"I'm sorry. I didn't think about how difficult it might be for you to get together with all your friends and not have your husband here with you." He got up from the sofa. "I'll be honest with you, Lana. I feel this crazy chemistry where you're concerned, but I also know it would be equally crazy to follow up on it. As you said, you're not the hook-up type, and that's really all I'd be interested in."

She nodded, his words merely serving to prove that her instincts were right. Riley Kincaid had heartbreak written all over his sexy self, and she'd already had enough of that to last a lifetime.

Wearily, she got off the sofa. "I'm going to bed."

"And I'm going in to check the camera film and see if I can spot what made the alarm ring."

Together they walked down the hallway and each went into their own separate rooms. It didn't take long for Lana to prepare for bed, and once she was beneath the covers she found her thoughts still filled with Riley.

It was true, it had been a difficult evening on a number of levels. She'd had to cope with the lies she was telling her neighbors and the fact that one of them was under FBI scrutiny for being a potential serial killer. She'd also endured memories of Joe and the realization that in many ways Riley reminded her of her dead husband. And that was even more of a reason that he was dangerous to her.

Joe had been a great guy, but beneath the charm he'd been an incredibly weak man. She'd loved him, but that didn't mean she wanted to hook up with anyone like him ever again.

Sleep was not restful when it finally came, and she welcomed the morning. She woke early and went in to check on Haley, who was still sleeping soundly, then followed the scent of fresh coffee to the kitchen.

"Good morning." Riley offered her a friendly but distant smile as he stirred a skillet of scrambled eggs. As usual, he looked totally hot in his worn, fitted jeans and a light-blue T-shirt and bare feet.

"That smells good," she said as she took a seat at the table.

"A few potatoes, some green peppers and lots of cheese," he replied.

"Want me to make some toast or something?" she asked.

"Nah. It's already made. Just relax. You'll need your energy for when Haley wakes up." He took the eggs, divided them between two plates with a couple of pieces of toast and joined her at the table.

"I'm not used to being waited on," she said as she picked up her fork.

He smiled. "It's just breakfast. I have to go to headquarters this morning. We're having a meeting about this case." He frowned and picked up a piece of his toast.

"Things aren't going the way you wanted them to?" she asked.

"The timeline we've been working with is that

there's been a murder every four weeks or so. We're now going into the sixth week and so we know something is probably going to happen, but needless to say the surveillance so far has yielded nothing."

"You haven't even been here a week yet. Maybe you're all expecting too much too soon?" She picked up her fork and stabbed a piece of scrambled egg.

"Maybe." He took a bite of his toast. "If I didn't know better I'd swear Greg knows he's under surveillance. Since I've been here he's been living his life like a monk, going to bed early, not socializing with anyone." He threw the toast down to his plate in disgust.

"Do you think he knows about us? That we aren't really married?" she asked worriedly, and set her fork down, the very thought banishing any hunger she might have felt.

"No, I think he bought it," he said hurriedly. "Maybe he just knows the heat is on and so he's being especially careful. He's been interviewed a number of times concerning these crimes. He has to know that he's at least on our potential suspect list. Anyway, I'll know more about what our next move might be after the meeting this morning."

They ate for a few minutes in silence, and Lana had just finished when Haley called out from her bedroom. Lana dressed her daughter, then gave her breakfast and decided to run a few errands before it got too warm outside.

"While you're at your meeting Haley and I are going to run out for a few groceries. Is there anything you need?"

"No thanks." He offered her a smile, but it was a distant one. "I'll walk out with you."

They walked out into the warm morning where both his car and hers were parked in the driveway. "Will you be home for lunch?" she asked.

"I don't know. Don't worry about me. If I run late I'll grab a burger on the way back." He smiled again, but the warm charm, the flirty gleam were gone. "I'll see you later."

He'd apparently taken their conversation from the night before to heart. He was keeping not only his physical distance but an emotional one as well. She told herself she wasn't going to miss that flirtatious light in his eyes or that sexy smile that caused a sizzling heat in the pit of her stomach.

As she walked with Haley to her car she glanced at the house next door, wondering what Greg had planned for the day. He was usually off on Saturdays and Sundays and often spent part of that time working in his yard or washing his car.

There was no sign of him as she buckled Haley into her car seat. "We're going to the store," she said to her daughter as she got in behind the steering wheel.

"If I'm good then I get a surprise?" Haley asked.

Lana smiled at her daughter in her rearview mirror. "We'll see." Which usually meant "of course." Lana was aware that she often spoiled Haley, but she was such a good little girl it was difficult not to spoil her.

Lana worried about her daughter growing up without a father. She knew the statistics that foretold promiscuity and early pregnancy for girls who didn't have a strong father figure in their lives.

Lana had lied to Riley when she'd told him she'd realized she wasn't ready for a relationship. She just wasn't ready for the kind of relationship he wanted—hot and sweaty and very temporary.

In another week or so he'd return to his life, and he would have no problem picking up where he'd left off with his other women. With his charm and good looks he could pick up a woman anywhere.

She tightened her hands on the steering wheel as old memories shifted through her mind. She steadfastly shoved them away. She couldn't think about Joe. He was gone, shot to death by an unknown assailant.

By the time she arrived at the grocery store Haley was ready to shop. "Cookies! Candy! Toys!" She eagerly clapped her hands together as Lana got her settled in the seat in the shopping cart.

"How about some lettuce and milk and bread?" Lana replied.

"Okay, milk," Haley agreed.

Lana started up the first aisle as she went over her grocery list in her head. As she picked up fresh produce to add to her cart, Haley smiled and chattered at the people who passed them.

Lana hadn't realized how tense the situation in her home had been until now, with the tension momentarily removed. The stiffness in her shoulders eased and her heart slowed as she filled her mind with nothing more than the scent of fresh melon and the ripeness of the cherry-red tomatoes.

Finished in the produce aisle, she moved to the next one and began to pick up canned goods. She was bent over to grab several cans of tomato sauce when she felt it—the creepy sensation of being watched.

She straightened and looked around, her uneasiness growing. She and Haley were alone in the aisle, but at the end she thought she saw somebody dart just out of sight.

She froze and gripped the handle of the shopping cart as her heart began to beat a frantic rhythm. Had somebody been watching her? Why would anyone be paying any attention to her? Or was she suffering from an overactive imagination?

"Mommy?" Haley gazed up at her, apparently sensing Lana's sudden burst of tension.

"It's okay." Lana forced a smile. "Let's go buy some cookies."

"I love cookies," Haley exclaimed. "Get cookies for Daddy, too."

"Honey, you know Riley isn't your daddy," Lana said.

Haley pursed her bottom lip in one of her infrequent pouts. "But I want him to be my daddy, so he is," she exclaimed.

Lana sighed. Haley was a good kid, but she could also be bullheaded, and by the look on her little face Lana knew there was no point arguing with her.

As she headed for the cookie aisle she looked at the people she passed, older women pushing carts, a group of firemen buying items to cook at the station. There was nobody around who looked threatening or sinister.

Still, as she reached for the box of cookies that were Haley's favorites, she felt it again. It was a chill that crept up her spine and pooled in the pit of her stomach. Once again she saw nothing and nobody that could account for the feeling.

Maybe she was under more stress than she'd realized, she thought as she headed for the checkout counters. She'd thought she'd been handling everything relatively well, but now she was feeling phantom stares from equally phantom people.

She prayed that it was just her imagination and nothing more sinister, but she breathed a small sigh of relief when she and Haley were back in the car with the doors locked.

Still, it was difficult to dismiss the fact that she was part of a game they were playing with a man suspected of murdering women just like her. And the game wasn't over yet.

Riley sat at a large table in a conference room at headquarters with six other agents and their supervisor on this particular operation. The topic of discussion had been the lack of information coming through their surveillance efforts.

"It's only been a week," Riley said, repeating what Lana had said to him earlier. "We definitely need to give it more time. It's the weekend, and maybe Greg will do something more interesting."

"All the murders occurred on weekdays," Frank Morrel replied. "So I doubt he's going to do anything too interesting."

"Has the profiler come up with anything resembling a motive for these murders?" Bill McDonald asked.

"You mean besides that fact that he's just a sick bastard?" Frank quipped.

"At least he has his standards. He doesn't kill the kids that are at the crime scenes," Roger Smith, one of the other agents replied.

"Thank God for small favors," Riley replied.

For the next hour they discussed what they'd learned about the murders already committed, talked about the victim profile and talked about what type of woman might be the next victim.

"What about the baby's breath?" Riley asked. It

had been the one piece of evidence they had managed to keep out of the media, that the killer left a sprig of baby's breath at each murder scene.

"In flower language it stands for innocence, but we haven't been able to find any literary reference or anything else that might make sense as to why our killer chose that to leave behind," Roger said.

"Maybe he thinks the women were guilty of something? Was there any indication they were cheating on their husbands?" Frank asked.

"Nothing that we could find in any of the cases," Roger replied.

Riley listened to the conversation going back and forth around the table. They were rehashing things that had already been discussed a hundred times, looking for angles they might have missed, suspects that could have been overlooked.

There was nothing more frustrating than knowing a man was guilty and not being able to prove it. And they all knew that Greg was guilty in some way where these murders were concerned.

It was close to noon when the meeting started winding down. "I suggest we give the surveillance a couple more weeks and see what happens in that time," Larry Carson, their supervisor, said.

Minutes later, as Riley headed back to Lana's house, he gripped the steering wheel tightly, his frustration twisting his guts.

He didn't want these murders to go unpunished.

Those women had been wives and mothers. His brain flashed with the memory that haunted his nightmares—the bloody kitchen and the dead woman on the floor.

Even though it had been years since her unsolved murder, the grief never went completely away. Nor did the lesson he'd learned on that horrible day.

He shoved the memories away as he turned down the street where he now lived. He sat up straighter in the driver seat as he saw four men with Greg playing basketball on Greg's driveway.

Adrenaline shot through Riley as he parked the car in Lana's driveway and went into the house. He assumed Haley was napping when he found Lana seated at the table with her jewelry in front of her.

"Hey!" she said as she looked up and saw him. "I didn't hear you come in."

He couldn't help the warmth that swept through him at her smile, and he hated that he was about to wipe it off her face. "I have a favor to ask you."

"What?"

"I want you to look out the window and see if you can tell me who is playing basketball at Greg's."

Her smile fell from her face, just as he'd known it would. She got up from the table and walked into the living room where from the side window she had a view of Greg's driveway.

"The kid in the red T-shirt and the one in the green striped shirt are Greg's nephews, but I don't know the other two." She moved away from the window as if afraid Greg might see her.

"His nephews?" Riley frowned. "According to our records Greg is an only child."

"From what he told me, his mother never married the man she lived with for a long time. That man had a daughter whom Greg considers his sister, and those are her two boys."

"Thanks." Riley went into his bedroom and changed clothes, then returned to the kitchen.

Her eyes widened as she saw the sports shorts and shirt he wore. "What are you going to do?" she asked.

He gave her a grim smile. "I'm in the mood to play a friendly game of hoops with the neighbor." He didn't wait to see what her response might be but instead headed out the front door.

Greg saw him as he walked across the yard toward his driveway. He grabbed the basketball and held it in his hands, a smile on his face.

"Hey, neighbor," Riley greeted him. "Saw the fun and wondered if you needed a sixth player."

"Definitely. That will give us two three-man teams," Greg replied. "Guys, this is my neighbor, Riley." Greg pointed a finger to a big man who appeared to be in his thirties. "Trent Clayton." He pointed to the next guy, another man who looked like he put the gym equipment to good use. "Seth Black." Finally he pointed to the two teenage boys.

"My nephews, Randy and Ricky Newsom. Why don't you take Trent and Ricky on your team, and my team will be Randy and Seth."

"Sounds good to me, although I should tell you it's been years since I've played," Riley replied.

"We aren't exactly the Dream Team," Ricky said, his voice slightly squeaky in the way of adolescence.

A jump shot gave the ball to Riley's team and it didn't take too much play for Riley to identify personality characteristics about the players.

Seth Black played almost brutally aggressively, more than once slamming an elbow into Riley's ribs and shoving him with more force than necessary. Trent was just as aggressive, although he didn't seem to take quite as much pleasure from the bodily contact as Seth did. The two teenage boys played well, although not with the intensity of the older men.

Riley memorized the names so he could give them to the office to check out. He couldn't remember any of these men's names coming up so far in their investigation.

They played two games with each team winning one, and then Seth said he had to get home. The rest of them went around the back to Greg's patio, where he cracked out cold beer for the adults and sodas for the two boys.

"For somebody who hasn't played in a long time, you're a pretty mean competitor," Trent said.

Riley smiled. "I like to win."

There was a hard glint in Trent's gaze. "Probably not as much as I like to win."

"Boys, boys," Greg said with an amused laugh. "I've never played a game that I didn't want to win. Life is just one big game."

Were these murders some sort of a perverse game for him? Riley took a sip of the cold beer despite the fact that his stomach was twisted into a knot of tension.

"We have to get home," Randy said as he finished his soda and crushed the can. As his older brother looked at him, Ricky quickly got out of his chair.

"Thanks, Uncle Greg, that was fun," he said.

Greg smiled. "You know the two of you are welcome here anytime."

The boys said their goodbyes and disappeared around the corner of the house.

"They seem like nice kids," Riley said.

"They're great kids," Greg replied with more than a touch of pride. "Straight-A students, involved in school activities and well liked by their peers."

"No thanks to their mother and that lowlife man she lives with," Trent said, and then looked at Greg. "Well, it's true. You have to admit that their mother isn't always there for them."

"Candy has some problems," Greg agreed easily, "but don't we all?"

The conversation turned to the weather and gym

workouts and other inconsequential subjects. It wasn't long before Trent stood. "I've got to get back to my hotel," he said. "I've got a meeting this evening."

"Oh, you're not from here?" Riley asked.

"Nah, I'm from St. Louis, but business brings me into town about once a month or so." Trent pulled his car keys from his pocket.

"So, how do you know Greg?" Riley asked.

The two men exchanged smiles. "We were buddies all through grade school and high school, so whenever I'm in town we get together."

"Well, it was nice meeting you," Riley said. "And it's time for me to head home, too."

With goodbyes said, Riley hurried across the lawn back to Lana's house, his blood filled with a surge of adrenaline.

Trent Clayton. There had been a darkness in his eyes, and he'd radiated a suppressed violence. He might just be the missing piece they'd been looking for, and if he was, then Riley's time at Lana's would be ending.

He should be glad. After all, he hadn't wanted the surveillance job in the first place. But surprisingly, he felt just a little sad at the idea of not seeing either Haley or Lana again.

They weren't his problem, he reminded himself. He was here to do a job, to catch a cold-blooded killer before he killed again. That was his job, and he'd do well to remember it.

Chapter Six

The cry woke Lana. It wasn't the high wail of Haley waking up but rather the low, harsh cry of Riley. In an instant she knew that he must be having another one of his nightmares.

She waited a moment to see if he'd awaken himself, but when the moans continued she got out of bed, pulled her robe around her and went down the hallway to his room.

In the spill of moonlight she could see him. He was on his back, writhing as if in physical pain as deep, tortured moans rasped from his throat.

"Riley."

She called his name from the doorway and he bolted up with a startled gasp, his eyes darting frantically around the room.

"Riley, are you okay?"

As he saw her standing in the doorway he released a deep, strangled sigh and reached over and turned on the lamp on the nightstand.

He looked haunted, the lines on his face etched deep into his skin and his hair askew. "Sorry, it was a nightmare." He wiped a hand down his face. "I didn't mean to disturb you."

She hesitated a moment. "You want to talk about it?"

"No. I don't know. Maybe," he amended. "Maybe if I talk about it I can finally get the damn thing out of my head."

She leaned against the door and waited for him to continue. He stared at the wall in front of him, his eyes filled with a darkness that threatened to consume him.

"I thought I'd outgrown the nightmare," he finally said. "I had it often when I was a teenager, but it eventually stopped for a while. These murders have brought it back." He drew in a deep breath. "I dream about my mother's murder."

She gasped. He'd told her his mother had died, but he hadn't said the woman had been murdered. He appeared fragile as he once again swiped a hand down his face. Before she knew it, she'd moved across the room and sat next to him on the bed.

He reached out and took her hand, as if needing a lifeline to hold on to before continuing. "It was just my mom and me. I told you my father walked out on us when I was young. He and my mother weren't married, and he left and we never heard from him again. Anyway, it was an ordinary June day. I was fifteen years old, and on that day instead of going straight home from school I hung out with some friends for about thirty minutes."

His fingers squeezed around hers and once again he stared at the wall. Even if he wasn't squeezing her fingers she would have been able to feel the tension that wafted off him like something noxious and heavy.

"It was Mom's day off, and the minute I walked into the house I knew something was wrong, but the full extent of how wrong didn't really hit me immediately. I could smell that she'd baked cookies, but there was something else, something bad in the air."

This time it was Lana who squeezed his fingers, hoping to give him the strength to revisit what must have been the most horrible experience in his life.

"I could smell the blood, the death in the air, but still I called out to her, telling myself everything was okay. Even when I saw a bloody handprint on the wall next to the kitchen my brain refused to accept what it meant." His voice deepened. "She was in the kitchen on the floor, and she'd been stabbed twenty-three times."

He turned and looked at Lana, and his eyes were filled with a teenage boy's horror, with a man's grief. "That's what I dream about. Only tonight there were two men there and both of them were taking turns stabbing her."

"Greg and Trent," she guessed.

He smiled, a gesture that did nothing to lighten the darkness in his features. "And the teddy bear goes to the lady in black." He pulled his hand from hers as the forced smile fell away. "I guess this case has stirred some old baggage."

"I'm sorry, Riley. Did they ever catch who was responsible for your mother's murder?"

"No. Nobody was ever charged with the crime."

"And what happened to you after that?"

"I became a ward of the state and went into the foster-care system. I got lucky and lived with a terrific family, Martha and Will Reynolds. Will was a police officer, and he was the person who helped me get into the FBI after college. I needed a positive way to vent my rage. I wanted to catch killers like the one who killed my mother."

Beneath his easy charm was far more substance than she'd initially thought. Even though she knew he was an intelligent man, that he would have to be smart to be an FBI agent, she'd thought him shallow, had guessed him to be self-absorbed and narcissistic.

He reminded her of Joe in so many ways. Big and solid and handsome as sin. And those weren't the only ways he reminded her of her husband.

Riley took her hand in his once again, and this time his smile held a bit of his overwhelming charm. "There is something to be said for nightmares that bring beautiful women into your bedroom. If you really want to erase the last of my bad dream, you could slide into bed with me."

Lana laughed, pulled her hand from his and then stood. "It's obvious you're feeling better. I'll see you in the morning."

"Good night, Lana. And thanks."

As she walked back down the hallway to her bedroom she saw the light in his room go out. He would probably find sleep quickly again, but she had a feeling sleep would be elusive for her.

Even though she knew Riley wasn't the man for her, there had been just a moment when she'd considered throwing caution to the wind and getting into bed with him.

As she slid beneath the sheets in her cold, lonely bed she thought about how long it had been since she'd been held, since she'd known the joy of lovemaking.

It had been almost two years since Joe's death, and even before he'd been killed, their sex life had been less than stellar. There was a box of condoms still in the nightstand on what had been his side of the bed. How easily she could pluck one out of the drawer and go back into Riley's bed.

She closed her eyes and imagined what it would be like to have his warm, firm skin pressed against hers, to feel his hands sliding down the length of her body.

He was a temporary pretend husband and, in any

case, not the kind of man she wanted to make more permanent, but did that prevent her from enjoying a night of passion with him?

He'd probably make love to her once and then not be interested in doing it again. Old insecurities surged up inside her. She hadn't been enough woman for Joe. She could never be enough for a man like Riley.

She finally fell asleep and dreamed of Riley's hot kisses and sweet lovemaking, and she awoke the next morning with an ache of want deep in the pit of her stomach.

She rolled over on her side, glanced at the clock and shot straight up. Almost nine! She never slept this late. Why hadn't Haley cried out? She was always awake by seven.

Without bothering with her robe, she raced from her room into Haley's only to discover the little girl wasn't in her bed.

Panic clawed through her as she ran down the hallway and into the kitchen, only to gasp in relief as she saw Haley in her booster seat happily eating scrambled eggs and Riley seated next to her at the table nursing a cup of coffee.

"You gave me a scare," she exclaimed.

"Sorry. I just thought it might be nice to let you sleep in a little this morning since you were so nice to me in the middle of the night." He grinned knowingly, as if he'd been privy to her dreams.

"Mommy, want some eggs?" Haley asked with a beatific smile.

"Yes, Mommy, you want Daddy to make you some eggs?" Riley asked with a lift of one of his dark eyebrows.

"You shouldn't encourage her," Lana said.

Riley shrugged. "It's kind of cute, and I should add that you're definitely more than cute in that nightgown."

Lana crossed her arms over her chest. "I thought we agreed you weren't going to flirt with me anymore."

He laughed, the low, sexy rumble stirring warmth inside her. "I don't remember agreeing to that, and besides, you might as well ask me to stop breathing. Face it, Lana, you are a woman made to flirt with and I'm just the man to do the job."

"You're incorrigible," she exclaimed.

"I've been called worse. Go on, take a shower and get dressed or whatever you need to do. Haley and I are in good shape here, aren't we?"

"Good shape," Haley replied with a happy nod as she scooped up more eggs.

It was twenty minutes later when Lana left her bedroom. She'd taken a quick shower, dressed, and felt ready to officially face the day.

Riley and Haley were in the living room seated on the floor and tossing a big blue ball back and forth. Each time Riley threw her the ball Haley released gales of giggles that shot straight through to Lana's heart.

Surely Haley was too young to truly bond with Riley. Surely it wouldn't take her long to forget the handsome man she called Daddy.

Lana had a feeling it would be far more difficult for herself to forget the handsome Riley.

"Fun time is over," Riley said as he got up from the floor. "I've got a meeting to attend." He tucked his shirt into his jeans. "Agent Morrel called to let me know they have some background on Trent Clayton, so I'm meeting him for lunch."

"Do you think he's the partner you've been looking for?" Lana asked as she sat on the edge of the sofa.

"Right now he's top on my list, but that doesn't mean he's guilty of anything more than rough ball play and picking bad friends. The good part is he's now on our radar and he wasn't before."

At that moment the phone rang and Lana answered.

"When were you going to tell me that you sneaked off to Vegas and married some hunk?"

It was Kerry Peters, Lana's best friend and the only person she trusted to babysit Haley. As Lana gave her friend the party line, Riley disappeared into the guest bedroom and Haley began to play house with her baby doll.

"I thought we told each other everything," Kerry exclaimed.

"We do. I was just keeping Riley a secret until I knew for sure it was going to work between us. I'd intended to tell you when I brought Haley over next Friday afternoon. You are still planning on keeping her for me, aren't you?"

"Of course, but I have to confess I'm a little hurt that I found out about your marriage from somebody other than you."

As Lana tried to make amends to her friend, she suddenly wondered what would happen in the next week or two when Riley suddenly disappeared.

If Greg still hadn't been arrested at that time, would she have to continue this charade? Would she then have to go through a pretend separation and divorce?

By the time she'd finished with the telephone conversation, Riley was back in the living room.

"That was my best friend, Kerry," Lana said to Riley. "She's going to watch Haley for the weekend so I can stay at the hotel where the jewelry show is taking place."

"That's this weekend?" he asked.

She nodded. "I usually leave here around noon on Friday and get back Sunday night."

"The whole weekend?"

"It's once a year and provides a lot of my living

expenses for the rest of the year. Anyway, I was just thinking about when you leave here."

"What do you mean?"

"I mean when this assignment is over for you, what am I supposed to tell people about you, about us?"

He sat on the sofa next to her. "If we have Greg under arrest, then you can tell everyone the truth, that you were a hero and came to the aid of the FBI. If Greg hasn't been arrested, then you can tell everyone that I turned out to be a bastard and you kicked me out of the house."

She frowned and he reached out and touched the freckles on her nose. "Make it easy on yourself, Lana. Make me the bad guy."

"That just doesn't seem quite fair. I mean, you haven't been a bad guy in all this," she protested.

He grinned. "Give me time. I'm not done here yet."

He got up from the sofa. "I'm going to take off. I've got a couple of errands to run before I meet Frank."

"Will you be home for dinner? I have a couple of steaks to grill." She realized how domestic they sounded, like a real couple going over the schedule for the day.

"Sounds great." He pulled his keys from his pocket.

"Bye, Daddy," Haley said. "Give me a goodbye kiss."

Riley bent down and kissed Haley on the forehead, then, with a goodbye, he was out the door.

As always there was a faint whoosh, as if the room's energy left with him. She was getting far too accustomed to having him in the house. When he left she was going to miss the easy conversation they shared, the laughter he pulled from her and the simmering possibility of passion that existed between them.

It was going to be difficult to go back to the loneliness that had plagued her before he'd arrived. She loved her daughter and many of the hours of the day were spent playing with Haley, but it was the evening hours after Haley had gone to bed when Lana had hungered for companionship and for something more.

She forced the thoughts from her mind and focused on her daughter, playing house until lunchtime. Afterward, she put Haley down for a nap.

Once Haley was asleep Lana returned to the kitchen, got out her jewelry and plugged in the soldering iron. She wanted to finish at least ten more pieces by the weekend show.

Usually, it was easy for her to lose herself in the creative and meticulous process, but today her mind refused to drift away from Riley.

The story of his mother's murder had shocked her, and her heart had ached for the boy who had lost so much. Was it possible that the loss of his mother had so scarred his heart that he now had the inability to love anyone else?

She now knew he was thirty-three years old and had never been married. According to him, he'd never even come close.

Did his easy charm and flirtatious ways hide a heart that was so damaged from his mother's death that he couldn't truly open it up to anyone?

She laughed at her own psychological skills. Joe had been charming and a flirt and there had been nothing damaging in his background. It was possible Riley just had no interest in being a family man.

What she didn't understand was why that made her ache more than a little bit. He was so good with Haley. He would make a wonderful father, but she wasn't sure he'd make such a great husband.

There were parts of this pretend marriage that felt all too real—Riley's affection for Haley, the easy daily routine they'd all fallen into and most of all the desire that was a shimmering energy between them. She consciously shoved these thoughts away as she forced herself to focus on the task at hand.

She didn't know how long she'd been working when she thought she heard what sounded like the front door open and close.

"I'm in the kitchen," she yelled, assuming it was Riley.

When there was no answer and he didn't appear in

the kitchen doorway, she set her soldering iron aside and got up from the table. "Riley?"

She left the kitchen and went into the living room, but there was nobody there. Her heart hammered suddenly as she thought about Haley. Had she awakened and gone outside? She'd never done anything like that before, but that didn't mean it couldn't happen.

She raced down the hallway and into Haley's bedroom and sighed in relief as she saw the little girl still sleeping soundly on her toddler bed. Thank God, Lana thought.

Maybe she'd just imagined the sound of the door. With a smile at her sleeping daughter she left the bedroom and went back down the hallway.

She walked back into the kitchen and sat at the table, then screamed as a man stepped out of her pantry, a ski mask covering his face and a knife clutched in his hand.

"How's it going with you and the little wife?" Frank said, grinning.

Riley sat back in the booth as his thoughts went to Lana. "Actually, it hasn't been too bad. She's been very cooperative and easy to get along with."

"She's cute. Too bad about her husband."

"Yeah, I think she's still mourning his death." Riley thought about those moments when he thought he saw grief and a fragile wistfulness in her eyes.

The two men were in a café in an area of downtown

Kansas City that had been refurbished with new nightclubs, restaurants and theaters. Down the street was Bartle Hall, the convention center where the jewelry show would be held that weekend.

"I don't think this surveillance crap is going to work," Frank said as he dipped a French fry into a pool of ketchup.

The café was busy, but the two men were seated in a red vinyl booth near the back where it was less noisy with diners.

"It gave us Trent Clayton," Riley replied.

"A nasty piece of work, but I can't see him working in tandem on murdering women. From reading his file he doesn't strike me as a man who'd be a partner in much of anything."

"Who knows what brings men together to kill? Murder can make strange bedfellows. Besides, you said Trent has a history of violence."

Frank nodded. "Three arrests on assault charges, all three of them the result of bar fights. The man obviously has a bad temper, especially after a couple of drinks."

"Has anybody checked his alibis for the days of the murders?" Riley motioned to the waitress for their tab.

"Being done as we speak. I hope he is our guy. I'd love to wrap up this case with a neat and tidy bow."

"Yeah, with Cary and Clayton both behind bars," Riley replied. His stomach clenched as he thought of the two men whom he believed preyed on women. "I just wish Greg would stumble so we could arrest him. Every time I watch him go to work in the morning I worry that he's picking his next victim."

"You know we've got agents in place to watch who he talks to, who he works with." Frank pushed his plate away and reached for his cup of coffee. "We're trying to keep any potential victims safe."

"Unless he breaks the pattern," Riley said with a frown. "All the previous victims came from the gym, but there's nothing to say he won't break his own pattern and just pick up a woman off the streets."

"You know we aren't going to let that happen if we can help it. Besides, the profiler has come up with a new twist as far as his victim pattern."

"And what's that?"

"It's something about newlyweds with kids. All the women had been married less than six months to men who weren't the fathers of their children. We think the baby's breath somehow symbolizes the innocent children in the blended marriage."

"That doesn't explain why he's killing their mothers," Riley said.

"Who knows? If we had all the answers we wouldn't be sitting here now talking about it."

As the waitress brought the tab Riley straightened in the booth. "If the criteria for a victim is that she has children and recently married a new man, then we just made Lana a perfect victim."

"Yeah, I guess you're right," Frank said, but his eyes didn't meet Riley's.

Riley felt anger stir inside him. "How long have you known about this particular victim profile, Frank?"

"A couple of days." Frank shrugged.

"Was this on purpose? Was the intent all along to use Lana as bait?"

"You're asking the wrong person these questions, Riley. I'm just a grunt like you. I just do what I'm told and don't ask questions."

Riley grabbed his wallet from his pocket and tossed out his half of the bill on the table. His stomach twisted in knots as he fought against his anger.

"It's time for me to head home so I can tell Lana we not only invaded her privacy and forced her to pretend to be married to me, but we also made her a perfect target for the psycho next door."

His anger chased him out of the restaurant and to his car, where he got in and then slammed his palm against the dash.

They'd known all along they could potentially be placing Lana in danger. And they went through with the ruse anyway.

As he drove home his irritation was a hulking passenger that filled the car. Why hadn't anyone filled him in on this detail? Didn't they think it was important for him to know that Lana might be in danger?

Maybe they didn't think she was in danger simply

because of her relationship with Greg. Surely he'd be a fool to make his next-door neighbor one of his victims.

By the time Riley pulled into the driveway he'd managed to calm himself down. Really, nothing had changed. He was still watching the creep next door and fighting an overwhelming desire for Lana.

He parked his car in the driveway, got out and stretched with his arms overhead as his gaze shot to the house next door.

Greg would be at work today, and he could only hope that what Frank had said was true, that agents were in place there to keep an eye on Greg's movements.

He walked up to the front door, noting that the grass needed cutting and the flowers were bedraggled from the heat.

He opened the front door. "Honey, I'm home," he yelled.

Lana's reply was a scream of terror that iced his blood as he raced for the kitchen.

Chapter Seven

At the sound of Riley's voice, the intruder opened the back door and fled from the house as Lana collapsed to the floor, sobs racking her body.

She was vaguely aware of Riley rushing into the kitchen, his gun in hand. She raised a finger and pointed toward the door. "He went out."

"Are you okay?" Riley asked, his voice laced with an urgency she'd never heard before.

She nodded. "Just go get him," she said between gasping sobs.

As Riley ran out the back door, she pulled herself up to a chair at the table. Her leg was bleeding, slashed in the fight for her life. Thankfully, it was a superficial wound, but the terror that still coursed through her had her heart feeling as if it might explode out of her chest.

Her soldering iron was on the floor and she bent down to pick it up. She'd tried to use it on him to keep him from hurting her, but he'd easily taken it away from her and thrown it aside.

If Riley hadn't arrived home at that very minute, she had no doubt that she'd be dead. Behind the ski mask the man's eyes had glittered with a bloodlust that had been terrifying.

She got up from the chair and hurried down the hallway to Haley's room. She sagged against the door as she saw that Haley was still asleep. Thank God.

The thought of Haley awakening and coming into the kitchen during the heat of the battle nearly cast Lana to her knees. She'd consciously not screamed while she'd fought him because she hadn't wanted that to happen.

Leaving Haley's doorway, she pressed her hand against the knife wound, where blood still oozed. She returned to the kitchen and got a wet cloth, then sat back down to clean the cut.

It could have been her throat he'd slit. Tears fell as she pressed the cloth against her leg. He'd tried to stab her several times but she'd somehow managed to stay just out of his reach.

Riley came in the back door, his frustration evident in the darkness of his eyes and the strain of his features. His gaze went to her leg and his eyes grew even darker. "You told me you weren't hurt," he growled as he crouched down in front of her.

"It's okay. It's not deep. You didn't catch him?"

He took the cloth from her and frowned. "No.

I've called it in and the police should be here anytime. Want to tell me what happened?" He wiped the
wound, which had finally stopped bleeding.

"I was working here at the table and I thought I
heard the front door open and then close. I called
out to you and when there was no answer I thought
maybe it was Haley. I went and checked on her but
she was still sleeping, and then I decided it was all my
imagination. When I went down the hallway to Haley's room he must have sneaked into the kitchen and
hidden in the pantry." Her words tumbled over each
other as the fear built up inside her once again.

"I sat at the table to get back to work and suddenly
he was there in front of me. He had on a ski mask and
he had a knife." An alien chill reached inside her to
encase her heart and she fought against the resulting
shiver.

Riley got to his feet and looked around the room.
She followed his gaze. Pieces of jewelry were on the
floor and the table was twisted sideways, evidence
of the struggle that had taken place. She frowned as
she saw a sprig of baby's breath on the floor. Riley
cursed beneath his breath.

"What's that?" she asked, a new fear welling up
inside her.

He was silent for a long agonizing moment that
only fed her fear. "That's the signature of our serial
killer," he finally said.

She stared at him as fear turned to horror. At that

moment Haley awoke from her nap and the police arrived at her door.

Within thirty minutes the police had left as the FBI took over the scene. Lana was questioned and her kitchen was dusted for prints. They swept the floor and gathered what they could in an effort to find something that might identify the intruder.

The baby's breath was bagged and tagged, and agents were in the neighborhood asking questions to find out if anyone had seen anything that might lead to an arrest.

Riley was out in the backyard with the man Lana assumed to be his supervisor, and occasionally she heard his voice rise in anger through the open back door.

Haley was delighted with all the company and walked from agent to agent asking them to play with her.

The horror had left Lana and had been replaced by a troubling numbness. She felt as if her head had been wrapped in cotton and nothing that was going on around her had anything at all to do with her.

It was after seven when Riley walked the last of the investigators to the door. Even though she knew she should get up from the sofa, do something constructive, she remained seated and in a crazy fog.

Riley closed and locked the front door and scooped up Haley in his arms. "Why don't you go take a hot shower," he suggested to Lana. "Haley and I will fix something for dinner."

"A shower sounds good," she agreed. She wanted to wash away the feel of his hands on her, his scent of sweat and madness that seemed to cling to her skin. "But I was going to do steaks on the grill for dinner."

"We can do steak another night. Go on, Lana. Take a hot shower and get ready for bed. It's been a long day."

She didn't argue with him but pulled herself up and drifted down the hallway to the bathroom. Minutes later, as she stood beneath a hot spray of water, the numbness began to ebb and she began to cry as she relived each and every moment of the attack.

She leaned weakly against the cold tiles of the shower wall as sobs ripped from her depths. Never had she known the kind of terror that she'd experienced when she'd seen him standing in front of her, the knife glittering in his hand.

All she'd been able to think of was Haley's safety. If she was killed, would the intruder then go after her daughter? She'd known she couldn't let that happen, that someway, somehow she had to survive.

Finally, she'd scrubbed her skin nearly raw and had no more tears left to cry. She shut off the water and dried off, trying to keep her mind from what had happened.

She pulled on her old oversize T-shirt, then

went back into the kitchen where Haley was in her booster seat and Riley was fixing grilled-cheese sandwiches.

The kitchen was back to normal. Her jewelry items had been cleaned up and packed away. The table was once again where it should be, and there was no evidence of what had occurred hours before.

"Tomato soup and grilled cheese," he said as she slid into a chair at the table. "The best comfort food in the world."

She needed comfort. An icy chill filled her as she looked at the back door to make certain it was locked. She could have been killed in this room. That had been the man's intention.

"Lana."

She jumped at Riley's sharp tone. "Look at me, Lana. You're safe now. I'm not going to let anything happen to you."

"Smile, Mommy, smile!" Haley exclaimed.

Lana straightened in the chair and forced a smile to her face. "I'm smiling," she said to her daughter. The last thing she wanted was to upset Haley in any way.

"You ready for some grilled cheese?" Riley asked Haley who nodded eagerly.

He cut the sandwich in fourths and laid it on her plate, then went back to the skillet to flip the two he had working.

Within minutes he'd finished up the sandwiches

and soup and had joined Lana at the table. "You need to eat," he said.

She dutifully picked up her spoon and lowered it into the tomato soup, but instead of raising it to her lips she looked at Riley. "What were you arguing about with that man in the backyard?"

"A little bit of everything. We can talk about it all later. Now you need to eat."

The warmth of the soup did nothing to banish the chill inside her, but she ate it and then carried her dishes to the sink. By that time Haley had finished eating and it was time for her bath.

Lana went through the motions of bath time and kept her mind empty of all thought or emotion. She leaned over the side of the tub and played with Haley in the water, then washed her hair and finally pulled her from the tub and dried her.

What she wanted to do was dress Haley, pack a bag and run away, but she knew no matter how far she ran she couldn't outrun the memories of those terrifying moments in the kitchen.

It was eight-thirty by the time she got Haley asleep for the night. She sat on the edge of the toddler bed and watched her daughter's little lips pucker with each breath she took.

Love swelled in Lana's chest along with the horror of how close she'd come to death. If she died, who would take care of Haley? Who would raise her and teach her all the things Lana wanted her to know?

Who would love her and make her feel safe and secure in a world where both her parents had been murdered?

Rachel was a wonderful woman and a loving aunt, but she and her husband had decided not to have children. They loved their carefree life without responsibility. Although they would do their best to love Haley, it wouldn't be the same.

You weren't murdered, she told herself as she got up from the bed. *Other than a cut on the leg you're just fine.*

She left Haley's room and found Riley in the living room, a cup of coffee in his hand and another cup on the coffee table in front of him.

"I made you some hot tea," he said, and gestured to the sofa next to him.

"Thanks." She sat next to him and wrapped her fingers around the hot cup. "I don't feel like I'll ever be warm again."

"You want to talk about it?"

She gave a shaky laugh. "I spent the whole night talking about it."

"You spent the whole night answering questions, giving facts. I thought maybe you might want to talk about how you felt, how you feel now."

She leaned back against the cushion and closed her eyes for several long moments. "It felt like it lasted a lifetime, from the moment I saw him standing in front of me and the time you yelled from the front door. It was an eternity."

She opened her eyes as he took her hand in his. His handsome features were soft, his gorgeous, long-lashed eyes filled with empathy.

"It wasn't Greg," she said. "He was taller than Greg."

"I know. Greg was at the gym. Could you see the color of his eyes?"

Shaking her head she squeezed his hand a little bit tighter. "No, all I can tell you about his eyes is that they glittered with evil." She shivered, and he threw his arm around her shoulder and pulled her closer to him.

She burrowed against his side, seeking his warmth, the assurance of his strong arm around her. "Do you think it was Trent?" she asked.

"We'll know more when Trent is questioned about his whereabouts," he replied. "But you don't have to worry about that. The agents who are working this case will do what they can to find out who came in here to attack you."

"What about the baby's breath? Tell me about it," she asked, even though she wasn't at all sure she wanted to know.

"It's his signature. At every murder scene we've found a sprig of baby's breath. I also found out a part of the victim profile that I didn't know before."

She felt his tension harden his muscles. "And what's that?"

"It seems nobody thought it important to tell me that all his victims had a few things in common."

"Like what?" She searched his face, his tension becoming her own.

"All the women had small children, and all of them had recently married a man who wasn't the father of the kids."

She continued to stare at him as his words slowly sank in. "So, when we introduced you as my new husband to Greg, I became the perfect victim." She began to tremble uncontrollably.

He pulled her closer against him. "I'm sorry. I didn't know. They didn't tell me about the victim profile. There are a lot of things about this case they haven't shared with me."

"Is that what you were angry about earlier?"

He nodded. "That and the fact that we've got agents all over this neighborhood and nobody saw somebody coming through your front door."

"So what happens now?" she asked, surprised by how small, how reedy her voice sounded. "Do you think maybe because it was a failed attempt they'll pick another victim?"

His eyes were dark as he held her gaze, and fear once again twisted in the pit of her stomach. "There's no way to guess what their reaction will be to this failure."

"So I could still be in danger?"

"It's possible they'll choose another victim, but it's also possible that somehow in their sick, twisted minds you've become the ultimate prize, the one who escaped once but who they are determined won't escape the next time."

How had this happened? How had she gone from a relatively happy single mother raising a beautiful daughter to a potential victim of a serial killer? She believed Riley. She believed that he hadn't known about the victim profile.

"Was it the FBI's intention all along to use me as some sort of bait?" she asked.

He hesitated a moment. "I don't know. That's what I accused my supervisor of, but he insisted they hadn't thought it through, that you were chosen because you live next door to Greg and because they thought you would be cooperative and for no other reason. They didn't think he'd target you. In any case, it doesn't matter."

She looked at him in disbelief. "Doesn't matter? That's easy for you to say," she exclaimed.

"It doesn't matter because nothing is going to happen to you," he said firmly. "I'm off surveillance."

She gasped and moved out of his arms. "Does that mean you're going to leave here?" She was stunned by how much she didn't want to tell him goodbye.

"It means the exact opposite," he replied. "I'm not

only going to stay here, but until these men are in jail or the danger has somehow passed, you've just earned yourself a twenty-four-hour-a-day bodyguard."

It was just after eight the next morning and Lana, Riley and Haley were in the kitchen having breakfast when the doorbell rang.

"I'll get it," Riley said. He leaned down and touched the butt of the gun he had shoved into his sock, then rose from his chair and headed for the front door.

He'd decided that the gun would be part of his wardrobe for the rest of his time here with Lana. There was no way anyone was going to sneak up on her again. Not on his watch.

Even though he'd had the entire night to process what had happened, he couldn't get the sound of her scream out of his head. If he hadn't come home when he had, there was no doubt in his mind that Lana would be dead right now.

And if you'd gone straight home from school that day you might have been able to prevent your mother's murder, a little voice whispered inside his head.

He shoved it away, knowing that it was guilt and, by the very facts of the case, wasn't true. His mother had been dead for four hours before he'd arrived home that dreadful day.

He reached the door, and a peek out the security

hole displayed Greg standing on the porch. A wild rage filled Riley. He wanted to rip open the door and smash the man in the face. He needed to throw him on the ground and beat the hell out of him. He did neither.

Opening the door, he plastered a pleasant smile on his face. "Hey, neighbor," he said in greeting. He kept the door firmly in hand and didn't invite the man inside.

"Riley," Greg said with a nod. "It looked like you had a lot of excitement last night. I thought I'd check and see if everything is okay here."

The bastard had balls, Riley would give him that. "Yeah, some creep broke in here yesterday afternoon when I was gone and Lana and Haley were here alone. We think it was some sort of a robbery attempt and maybe he didn't know Lana was home. She confronted him and I got home before a real tragedy could occur. The gutless wonder ran out the back door and got away before I could catch him."

Greg frowned and shook his head as if in disgust. "You think you live in a safe neighborhood and then something like this happens. Was Lana able to identify the man?"

"No, he had on a ski mask."

"Maybe it was one of the neighborhood teenagers. I think we have several in the area who are dabbling in drugs. You know those dope addicts will rob anyone at anytime."

"The police gathered enough evidence that I think they'll be able to make an arrest in the next day or two," Riley said. *Chew on that, you bastard*, he thought.

"What kind of evidence?" Greg asked. Although his tone of voice remained light, Riley didn't miss the almost imperceptible tension that straightened his shoulders.

"Oh, I don't know. I didn't pay much attention to that end of things. I was just grateful that Lana and Haley were okay," Riley replied.

"I guess all's well that ends well, right?" Greg took a step backward. "I just wanted to make sure that everything was all right here."

"Everything is fine," Riley assured him, hoping his hatred wasn't showing in his eyes.

"Tell Lana I said hello, and I guess I'll see you later." Greg turned on his heel and left the porch.

Riley shut the front door and then moved to the window, where he watched Greg cross the yard to his own.

Greg walked several steps, then paused there and turned back to look at Lana's house. Riley stepped back from the window, but even from this distance he felt a malevolence rolling off the man.

Greg finally walked toward his house and disappeared inside. If only he could be arrested for the dark thoughts Riley knew were inside his head. If only they could get the evidence they needed to put the man and his partner behind bars.

He turned to see Lana standing just inside the living room. Her eyes were bigger than normal, and he could almost hear the pound of her heart. "He's gone," Riley said, and saw her swallow.

"What did he want?"

Riley walked over to her and placed an arm around her shoulder. "He said he saw the commotion over here and wanted to make sure everything was okay, but I think he was fishing to see what we might know."

She smelled wonderful, like something flowery and clean, and he realized it was a scent that he would always identify with her and with a simmering edge of desire that filled him.

"What you need to remember is that we have lots of agents working this case, and sooner or later Greg and his partner are going to make a mistake. Sooner or later we're going to get them, Lana."

She nodded and moved out of his embrace. He followed behind her as she returned to the kitchen and sat back down at the table. "He had a lot of nerve coming over here."

"Mommy, I want more toast," Haley said.

"Here you go." Riley picked up a piece of uneaten toast from his plate and handed it to Haley, who gave him a smile to melt his heart.

Like the woman across from him at the table,

the kid was getting to him as well. As crazy as it sounded, as much as he didn't want it to be so, they had come to feel like his family.

He hadn't expected the emotional toll this mock marriage would have on him. He'd thought he'd be able to breeze through it all with no scars left behind when he moved on, but he'd been wrong.

"You never told me where you really live," Lana said suddenly.

It was obvious she didn't want to talk about Greg anymore, didn't want to discuss the case. Riley moved to the counter and poured himself a fresh cup of coffee, then returned to the table to sit across from her.

"I have a small apartment downtown, although I'm not there too often." The apartment had never felt like home. It was just the place he went to eat and sleep when not working. No place had ever felt like home since the murder of his mother. He took a sip of his coffee and saw that she was slowly beginning to relax. It surprised him, how much he'd come to know about her, how easily he was beginning to read her moods.

"In your work do you do a lot of traveling?"

"Not a lot," he replied.

"What kind of case were you working when you got shot?" Her gaze went from his face to his shoulder.

"It was a gang-related issue. I went to talk to a man

we thought might have ties to the gang. He worked in the mayor's office as a clerk. I didn't expect anything violent, but when I showed up on his doorstep he pulled a gun and shot me." He shook his head as he remembered that moment of stunned surprise and pain. "It was my fault. I was careless in not being prepared for anything."

"I don't remember seeing anything about it in the papers," she said.

"We kept it out of the news at the mayor's request. The shoulder wound is what got me assigned to this surveillance case. The last thing I wanted was to be stuck on desk duty."

"And now you're on bodyguard duty."

He smiled in an attempt to lighten the mood. "And what a body it is."

Her cheeks pinkened but a tiny smile curved her lips. "You're terrible."

"Terrible," Haley echoed and laughed.

Lana's smile lasted only a moment and then faded. "It would be nice if this case was solved before this weekend," she said with a sigh.

"This weekend?" He looked at her curiously.

"My jewelry show, remember?"

God, with everything that had happened he'd forgotten all about the big show she'd planned on working. "Lana, I really don't think it's a good idea to go to the show."

She raised her chin and narrowed her eyes. "Don't tell me that. I don't want to hear it."

He looked at her helplessly. "Being out in a public place like that just isn't a good idea at this time in the game. It would be a logistic nightmare to try to keep you safe."

"You don't understand. I've worked most of the year to get things ready for this show." Her voice trembled slightly, but she lifted her chin in a show of defiance. "It's one of the biggest shows of the year. This is my business, Riley, this is important to me."

"There will be other shows," he replied, and instantly knew it was the wrong thing to say. Her eyes flashed with a fire of anger that he'd never seen before as she scooted her chair back from the table.

"Other shows? Like I said, this is one of the biggest ones in the Midwest. This is how I make my living." She got out of the chair as if unable to sit a moment longer. "You people have shoved your way into my life, disrupted my routine and placed me in danger."

"Are we having our first lover's quarrel?" he asked in an attempt to lighten her mood.

She scooped up Haley from her booster seat and turned back to face him. "You aren't my lover and I'm going to that show. It's up to you to make sure that I stay safe. That's what bodyguards do."

She didn't wait for his reply, but left the kitchen,

and a moment later he heard the door to Haley's bedroom slam shut.

Whew, she was pissed. He couldn't say he blamed her. She was right. They had all barged into her life and pretty well screwed it up.

He should be irritated with her, but instead a new respect for her filled him. She wasn't going to let Greg or the FBI push her around any longer. She was going to go to that jewelry show, and all he had to do was figure out how he intended to keep her safe in a crowd where he wasn't even sure who might be the danger.

He wouldn't confess it to anyone, but he was more than a little afraid for her, more than a little worried that no matter what arrangements they made, he wouldn't be able to keep her safe.

Chapter Eight

It was early Friday afternoon when Riley pulled up into Kerry Peters's driveway. Kerry and Lana had been friends since high school. She was divorced and had a five-year-old daughter, and the two women often took turns babysitting for each other.

Even though Haley was excited about staying with Kerry and her daughter, Kim, Lana worried that she'd been wrong to insist on going to the jewelry show for the weekend.

As Riley shut off the car engine, Kim came running out of the neat little ranch house, followed closely by her mother.

"Haley!" Kim cried, and danced in the yard next to the car with excitement.

"So, you're the new man," Kerry said as she smiled at Riley. "And you," she said, pointing a finger at Lana, "are in my doghouse for waiting so long to tell me about him."

Lana made the official introductions and then

hugged her friend as Riley got Haley out of her car seat. The two little girls squealed and hugged each other.

"We're going to play house and we'll play school and you can be the teacher and we'll make cookies and everything," Kim exclaimed.

"Are you sure you're up for this?" Lana asked her friend with a laugh.

Kerry smiled. "Are you kidding? It's always easier on me when Kim has a playmate. We'll be fine. You just go off with your handsome new hubby and sell a million dollars' worth of jewelry."

"Ah, from your lips to God's ears," Lana replied. She pulled a small suitcase from the backseat of the car and set it on the ground. "Here's everything you should need for her until Sunday. We should be here around six to pick her up. You have the number where we'll be?"

A hundred worries flittered around in Lana's head. What if Haley woke up in the middle of the night and cried for her? What if Greg managed to get to her despite Riley's protection and this was the very last time she'd see her daughter?

She knelt down and grabbed Haley to her, drawing in the sweet scent of babyhood that still clung to her. She hugged her tight, as if this might be the last time she held the person she loved more than anyone else in the world.

"Mommy, go," Haley said as she squirmed to get

free from Lana's embrace. "Me and Kim have stuff to do."

"Yes, go," Kerry exclaimed. "Don't worry, we'll be fine here."

Reluctantly, Lana released the wiggly Haley and stood. "Thanks, Kerry."

"Oh, don't thank me yet," she replied. "I have a ski trip planned in a couple of months and will be looking for a place for Kim for a few days."

Lana smiled. "You know we'd love to have her."

"And pencil me in for lunch next week. We need to have a long chat about Mr. Wonderful here," Kerry said, pointing at Riley.

"Today Mr. Wonderful, tomorrow just another downtrodden husband," Riley replied good-naturedly.

With final goodbyes said, Riley and Lana got back into the car.

Lana stared out the passenger seat and watched as Kerry and the two little girls disappeared into the house.

"Are you okay?" Riley asked as he backed out of the driveway.

"I'm fine," she replied, and cast him a quick glance. The past week had been a difficult one. After she'd thrown her temper fit about attending the show and had stomped out of the kitchen with Haley, he'd come into Haley's room and told her that they would go, that somehow he'd figure it out.

Things had been a bit tense between them since then. She'd spent the rest of the week working frantically to get as much of her jewelry finished as possible while he'd wandered from room to room like a caged animal seeking escape.

This morning as they'd packed the car with everything she would need for the weekend, she'd once again felt that creepy-crawly feeling that somebody was watching her. Watching them. More than once as they'd packed the car her gaze had drifted toward Greg's place, but she hadn't seen him anywhere around.

"It's a nice day," Riley said, breaking the silence that had filled the car.

"It's beautiful," she agreed. The intense heat that had marked the week had been swept away by a cool front that had the temperature hovering around the seventy-five degree mark. "Hopefully, a lot of people will get out tomorrow to enjoy the weather and will wind up at the show."

He looked relaxed and sexy in a pair of jeans and a navy blazer, but she knew the jacket hid his shoulder holster and gun. The gun was a reminder to her that while she was trying to sell her jewelry, Riley would be looking for somebody who wanted her dead, somebody who had partnered in an unholy alliance with her neighbor.

The most frightening part about the whole thing was that she didn't know whom to fear. She didn't know what face her killer might wear. She knew to be afraid of Greg, but until the FBI identified his partner, she couldn't know what other man might bring danger to her.

She knew Riley worried about the same thing. Every man who approached her booth would be scrutinized as a potential threat. It was going to be an exhausting weekend for them both.

"Thanks for doing this," she said.

He cast her a quick smile. "You didn't leave me much choice. You seemed pretty adamant that we were going to do this no matter what the consequences."

"You could have put your foot down, told me that if I wanted to come I was on my own," she replied.

"I couldn't do that," he protested. "Besides, you were right. We've taken enough from you, and I wasn't willing to take this away, too."

"Thank you," she repeated simply, knowing the words weren't adequate for what she was feeling but that they were all she had.

"Don't thank me now. We haven't survived this weekend yet. I'll expect you to be overwhelmingly grateful to me when we're back home." He raised an eyebrow with a mock leer.

She laughed, grateful that the tension between them had eased. Then she sobered. "But I know you were angry that I refused to stay home."

"I wasn't angry at you. I was angry at the situation,"

he explained. "I'm sorry we got you into this mess. I'm sorry that you were attacked in your own home." His gaze drifted to her calf where the wound she'd gotten was healing. "And I'm sorry I didn't catch the bastard who sliced you."

"It could have been worse," she replied. But she was aware that it wasn't over yet.

It didn't take long to arrive at the convention-center parking garage, where Riley pulled into a spot and demanded she stay in the car while he got out. She watched him as his gaze swept the general area, his hand on the butt of his gun.

She trusted him like she'd never trusted another man, at least to keep her safe. He apparently didn't see anything that caused him alarm, for he walked over to get a large dolly and then returned to the car and motioned her out.

It took them several minutes to load the large tubs and items from the trunk onto the dolly, and the whole time they worked Riley continued to look around as if anticipating trouble.

He didn't appear to relax until they entered the convention-center room where the booths were set up, and then he seemed to relax only a little bit.

"I'm in booth twenty-seven," she said. "It's at the end of the second aisle." She was pleased to have an end booth, which often got more traffic than the middle booths. Within an hour the room was a den of activity, with designers setting up their booths and checking out their competitors' wares.

Lana was aware of Riley's tension growing with each minute that passed, with each person who joined the chaos in the room. She tried to focus on setting up her booth, on the pleasure of seeing her pieces displayed against the deep-purple velvet she used as a backdrop, but it was hard to stay focused with Riley hovering around her.

She was not only aware of the growing tension in him but also the heady scent of clean male and slightly spicy cologne that clung to him and the welcome heat of his body whenever he was near.

By the time the doors opened to admit the general public, Lana was as much on edge as Riley appeared to be, but her anxiety was less about the fact that somebody might be after her and more about the fact that within mere hours she would be sharing a hotel room with Riley.

She felt fairly safe in the gathering crowd, thinking that Greg and his partner wouldn't be foolish enough to try anything here where there were so many potential witnesses.

She felt distinctly unsafe about sleeping in the same room with Riley, perhaps because she'd acknowledged to herself that maybe a simple hook-up with him wasn't such a bad idea after all.

As people began to fill the room, Riley moved behind her front table to stand next to her. She glanced at him and frowned as she saw his narrowed eyes, the lines of his face taut and pulled into a forbidding frown.

"If you don't relax a little bit you're going to scare any potential buyers away from my booth," she said. "You look like you could snap at any moment."

"Sorry," he replied and smiled. "I'll try to look more inviting."

She averted her gaze from him. Jeez, if he looked any more inviting she'd be tempted to jump his bones right now. What was wrong with her? Why was she thinking about getting Riley into bed, about making love to him, when she knew there was no future with him?

She'd read somewhere that often when in danger or believing they were facing death people wanted to have sex as a way of reaffirming life.

Maybe her feelings for Riley were really nothing more than the fear that she might die before she was held in a man's arms again, before she experienced the pleasure of lovemaking once more.

As a couple walked up to her booth she shoved those thoughts out of her head and focused on what she'd come here for—selling jewelry.

Riley felt like he might shatter at any moment. No job he'd ever done felt as nerve-racking as protecting Lana.

With each minute that passed the room became

more and more crowded with people coming far too close to her for his comfort. As he kept her in his personal space, another kind of tension built with every minute that passed.

Desire.

It slammed into him with the fruity scent of her shampoo, the crisp, clean fragrance of her perfume and the smile that lit her features each time somebody approached her booth.

When he'd first met her he'd believed she wasn't his type of woman, that her fresh-faced beauty wasn't the kind that moved him in any way, but he'd been wrong. So very wrong.

He found her shiny blond hair enticing and the sparkle in her eyes enchanting. And he didn't even want to think about how the swell of her breasts against her blouse and the shapeliness of her legs beneath her skirt affected him.

But his desire for her stemmed from more than her physical appeal. Over their time together he'd come to know her better than any woman he'd known in his life. He respected her inner strength and the way she mothered Haley.

When he was around her he felt a kind of peace he'd never known before. She was as comfortable as an old shirt and yet as exciting as a new exotic sports car. When she laughed he felt as if finally everything was right in the world.

All of these feelings combined with his need to

keep her safe, to make sure that he got her out of this mess not only alive but okay both mentally and physically.

"The necklace not only has earrings to match, but also a bracelet," Lana said as she showed a well-dressed woman the set. "As you can see, the pattern is a takeoff of autumn leaves."

She was a good salesman, not pushy but displaying her own love of her items, and that seemed to be the best selling point of all.

She not only shared with the potential customers what her inspiration had been while designing a particular piece but also the meaning of the stones and gems she used to create it.

Business was brisk and Riley remained on guard, making sure nobody came too close to her. He wanted to believe that the fact that they were in the middle of a crowd would keep her safe, but he knew better. In the crush and chaos of a crowd a perpetrator could kill and easily disappear among a sea of faces.

There were other agents in the area also keeping an eye on the crowd and on Lana, but Riley had no idea where they were or how close they might be if trouble arrived. He'd caught a glimpse of Frank Morrel earlier, but at the moment the agent was nowhere in Riley's sight.

At seven-thirty she called her friend's house to bid Haley good night. As she spoke to her daughter her features radiated with love, and Riley felt a swell in his heart as he thought of little Haley with her bright smile and happy laugh.

He'd never thought about having kids before, but if he ever had a daughter he hoped she would be as sweet and loving as Haley.

By eight o'clock the crowd had begun to thin and Riley felt some of the tension in his muscles begin to ease. With fewer people coming to the booth he had less to worry about. He sat on the folding chair next to hers and breathed a deep sigh.

"You okay?" she asked. Her eyes shone with a brilliance that nearly stole his breath away, and her cheeks were flushed with a charming color. The sales had been brisk, and it was obvious she was happy.

"I'll be fine when it's just the two of us in the hotel room, safe and sound," he replied.

"Maybe we can order in a late supper. We didn't stop to eat anything, and I'm hungry."

So was he, but unless the menu offered Lana à la carte he doubted he would find anything on it to satisfy his hunger.

She got up as a gentleman approached the front display table and Riley followed her, far too close to be a mere shadow.

By the time nine o'clock had arrived Riley felt as if he'd been on bodyguard duty for days. Every muscle in his body ached with the tension that had kept him hyperalert for the past several hours. He couldn't believe they were going to do this all over again tomorrow. And it would be a longer day. He stifled a groan at the thought.

"I just need to pack all this up in my jewelry case so we can take it all with us to the hotel room," she said as she began picking up the items and placing them in the rolling carrier.

"I can help. I promise I'll be careful."

She turned and smiled at him, the smile sending a shockwave of heat through him. "I'm trusting you with my body. I think I can trust you with my jewelry," she said.

When she smiled at him like that he was the last man she should be trusting with her body.

They began clearing the front display table first.

"It looked like you had a good evening," he said as he picked up a heavy, attractive bronze necklace. "It seemed like everyone who came to the booth bought something."

She laughed and reached across him for another necklace. "Not everyone, but it was a pretty good day."

She had no idea that her smile, the sound of her laughter only increased the tension inside him. The fact that she was so unaware of her own desirability only increased his desire for her.

When they'd finished clearing off the front table he turned to the one on the side and froze. Nestled between a hand-painted chunky bracelet and a matching necklace was a sprig of baby's breath.

Instantly his hand went to the butt of his gun and his gaze shot around the area, but there was nobody nearby for him to fear.

"Riley?"

Lana's voice came from somewhere behind him. "Is everything all right?"

He whirled around to face her, his heart pumping with a new burst of adrenaline. "No, everything isn't all right. Let's get these things together and get out of here."

She stepped up next to him. "What's wrong?" Her gaze fell on the baby's breath and she gasped, the color in her cheeks fading away as she clutched Riley's arm. "When did that happen?"

"I don't know, but we're packing up and getting out of here. I knew this was a bad idea." Dammit, he hadn't seen anyone in particular in the sea of faces that had passed through. Whoever had placed the flower there must have done it when there was a crowd around the table.

"Calm down," she said softly as the color began to return to her cheeks. "I am definitely not leaving. We're going to finish packing up my things and we're going to go to the hotel room and then tomorrow morning I'll be right back here. He doesn't get to win. Do you hear me, Riley? This was just a stupid attempt to scare me and I refuse to let him win." Her voice rang with anger as she clutched his arm.

He drew in a deep breath and released it slowly, allowing himself to do as she asked, to calm down.

She dropped her hand and took a step back from him. "For all we know he paid some kid to put that there. His goal was to frighten me, and he's probably sitting at home now gleefully waiting for us to pull back in the driveway." She shook her head and began to finish packing the last of the jewelry items.

"Nobody is going to take this weekend away from me. Not you, not the FBI and definitely not Greg Cary," she exclaimed. "We don't even know for sure if he's responsible for all this."

He watched her work for a moment. What he'd like to do was whisk her off to some foreign land where Greg or whoever couldn't touch her, but she wouldn't agree to that any more than she intended to agree with him about heading back to the house tonight.

And what if they all were wrong? What if it wasn't Greg after all? Then he had no idea whom to keep away from her, who might be responsible.

He had worked hard all his life to make sure he never cared about anyone. But somehow this slender blonde with her freckles and smile had dug deep under his defenses.

It scared him, the fact that he cared about her. It scared him almost as much as the idea of Greg somehow getting to her.

He certainly had no illusions of a happy ending

where they were concerned. She'd already made it clear to him that she was still grieving for the husband she'd lost. The right woman at the wrong time. It was just his luck.

By nine-thirty everything was packed, and together they left and headed across the street to their hotel.

Riley didn't relax again until he'd unlocked their hotel-room door and ushered her inside. He instantly claimed the bed closest to the door by throwing his duffel bag on top and then motioned her to the one on the other side of the nightstand.

"The first thing I'm doing is calling for room service," she said as she sat on the edge of the bed closest to the phone. "I'm getting a burger. Would you like something?"

Something? Oh yes. With just that simple question she'd set him on fire. Maybe it was the fact that they were in a room where the focal point was the two beds. The lighting was low, the mood was intense, and all he wanted was to stretch her out across one of the beds and make love to her until dawn.

"Riley?" Her cheeks flamed, and he realized he'd been staring at her.

"A burger sounds fine."

He walked over to the window and pulled the curtain aside to stare out on the darkened streets below as she placed the order.

"I'm going to go take a quick shower," she said as she hung up the phone.

"Okay," he replied, but didn't turn from the window. He didn't want to think about her standing naked beneath a hot spray of water. He didn't want to fantasize about the slide of the soap against her skin.

What he needed to do was call Larry Carson and tell him that despite the fact there were agents in the room, in spite of Riley's vigilance, somebody had placed baby's breath on the table.

How had they missed it? Even as the question filled his head he knew the answer. There had been dozens of people surrounding Lana's tables at times, so it would have been easy for somebody to surreptitiously drop the flowers on the table.

It had been a promise, an acknowledgment that although she'd managed to escape the first time, she was still their intended target. And that meant she was still marked for death.

Chapter Nine

Lana stood beneath the shower and tried to fight the feeling of impending doom. The sight of that flower had shaken her up more than she'd admitted to Riley.

It was a reminder that they hadn't forgotten about her, that they were still watching and waiting for the perfect opportunity to get to her.

Still, the one thing she didn't want to do was play their game. Logically she knew it had been an attempt to terrify her. They wanted her to run home with her tail tucked between her legs, and she refused to do that.

She turned off the water and grabbed the towel awaiting her on the edge of the sink. As she dried off she thought about Greg and the man who might be his partner. What kind of dynamics brought two men together to kill?

For that matter, what kind of dynamics brought two people together in love?

As she dried off she thought about her late husband. She knew all the qualities that had drawn her to Joe. He was bigger than life, with a sexy grin that made a woman feel as if she were the most important woman in the world. He'd been a charmer, a shameless flirt who had been a favorite at every party, in every social gathering.

In so many ways Riley reminded her of him. He had the same sexy, larger-than-life quality, his eyes sparkled with the same flirtatiousness, and when he smiled at her she felt as if she were the only woman on the face of the earth.

Wrapping the towel around her she grabbed her hairbrush and faced the mirror. As she worked the tangles from the wet strands, she tried to shove all thoughts of Greg and murder out of her mind.

She was pleased by her sales this evening and anticipated selling four times as much the next day. The money she earned should be enough to last until the Christmas holiday sales began in November.

Finished with her hair, she pulled a tube of scented lotion from her overnight bag and began to apply it to her bare skin.

She suddenly realized what she was doing—she was stalling. She told herself it was silly to be nervous to leave the bathroom. She'd already shared a bed with Riley when her sister had been in town. Besides, there were two beds in the next room, so it wasn't like she was going to be trapped in the same bed with him.

There was one problem. A part of her wanted to be trapped in bed with him. She knew it was a stupid thing to want, that he could never be the right man for her, but she wanted to be wrong for one night and throw caution to the wind.

She jerked as a soft knock sounded at the door.

"Burgers are here," Riley called out.

"I'll be right out." She quickly pulled on the demure nightgown and robe she'd brought with her. Her intention was to eat and then go straight to sleep. Tomorrow would be a long day, and it was in her best interest to get a good night's rest.

She belted her robe tightly around her and then left the bathroom. Riley was seated at the small table in the corner of the room. He'd unloaded their food and pushed the room-service cart against the door.

"Hmm, smells wonderful," she said as she slid into the chair opposite him.

She'd hoped he would relax once they got into the room, but he seemed even more tense now than he had earlier.

"I talked to Agent Morell, and none of the agents in the area noticed anyone placing that baby's breath on your table," he said.

"That doesn't surprise me. There were several times that the booth was crowded enough that nobody could really have seen what was going on."

She picked up one of her fries and popped it into her mouth.

"But it's their job to see what's going on," he said with a touch of irritation. "I've made sure that tomorrow the agents on duty stay closer to us than they did tonight. I also want you to tell me if anyone makes you feel the least uncomfortable, if for any reason you feel the slightest bit uneasy. You know that creepy-crawly feeling you sometimes get when you think somebody is watching you? That can be a genuine body response to potential danger. Don't dismiss it."

"I did," she said. "That morning that Haley and I went grocery shopping I had the feeling that somebody was watching me, but I kept dismissing it as my imagination. When I think back now I think maybe I saw Trent in the store with me." She fought against a shiver at the idea that he'd been so close to not just her, but to her baby.

"Are you sure?"

She hesitated a moment and then shook her head. "Not a hundred percent sure."

"You should have told me about it," he admonished her.

"I would have but I thought it was just my imagination working overtime."

"Don't ignore it again," Riley said.

"I promise I won't," she replied. "And now we'd better eat before this all gets cold."

For the next few minutes they ate in silence. Lana couldn't begin to guess what thoughts were going through his mind. He seemed closed off in a way she'd never seen. His green eyes were like the murky waters of a mossy pond, impenetrable and mysterious.

Maybe he was angrier than she'd realized that she'd insisted they come here. Certainly his job as a bodyguard was more stressful here than it would be if she'd just stayed home.

She didn't say anything until they'd finished eating and he'd pushed the room-service cart with all their dirty dishes out into the hallway. Then she moved from the chair to the edge of her bed and gazed at him.

"I wouldn't blame you if you're angry with me for forcing your hand in coming here," she said softly. "I know I could have made things much easier on you by not coming."

"What makes you think I'm mad?" he asked.

She offered him a small smile. "We could start with that muscle that's overworking itself in your jaw and the rigid set of your shoulders. Then there's the fact that you've hardly spoken to me since we came in here."

"I'm not mad." His voice was clipped as he took off his blazer and then removed his gun and holster and set it on the top of the nightstand.

"You sound mad," she replied.

He faced her, his eyes simmering with a fire that stole her breath away. "Lana, the only thing I'm feeling right now is the frustration of a man who wants you almost as much as he wants to draw his next breath. I can't remember the last time I wanted a woman as badly as I want you, and right now I'm doing everything in my power to hang on to my self-control. In fact, I'm going to take a shower. A very cold shower." He practically ran for the bathroom and closed the door with more force than necessary.

She stared at the closed door, a swell of heat rising up and sweeping over her entire body. He wanted her. He wanted her badly.

As she replayed his final words in her mind, a sweet shiver raced through her. She wanted him, too. She didn't care that he wasn't the man who would be with her at the end of her life. It was enough that he would be the man in bed with her in the morning.

Without giving herself a chance to change her mind, she unbelted her robe and pulled it off, then removed her nightgown. Wearing only a pair of panties, she pulled down the heavy gold bedspread on his bed and slipped in beneath the sheets.

She lay there and gave herself time to change her mind, to quickly jump back up and get into her own bed. But there wasn't a doubt in her mind. She was exactly where she wanted to be.

When she heard the water stop running in the bathroom, a new shiver of anticipation whispered through her. She knew if she were going to change her mind, now was the time to do it, before he stepped out of the bathroom door.

Rather than jumping out of the bed, she snuggled deeper, feeling a crazy sense of rightness in this moment. She had no idea what tomorrow might bring, but tonight she was going to sleep in Riley's arms.

The bathroom door opened and Riley stepped into the doorway and froze. Even though he was backlit by the bathroom light, she could not only see that he wore nothing but his jeans, but she could also see the wild glitter in his eyes.

"Lana, you're in the wrong bed," he said, his voice a husky whisper.

"I'm exactly where I want to be," she replied.

He remained frozen for several long moments. "Are you sure?" he finally asked.

"I've never been so sure of anything in my life. Turn out the light and come to bed, Riley."

The bathroom light winked off, leaving only the faint spill of illumination from the nightstand lamp, enough light for her to see the hunger that claimed his features as he pulled his wallet from his back pocket and laid it next to his gun on the nightstand.

She wanted to do it right. She wanted to be enough for him, at least for this night. There had been so many times in her life when she'd felt as if she hadn't been enough.

Her heart beat so loud, so fast she wondered if he could hear it thundering in the room when he took off his jeans, leaving him only in a pair of navy briefs.

He slid beneath the sheets and she held her breath, waiting for him to reach out to her, to touch her. "Are you sure you know what you're doing? I don't want you to regret this in the morning." His voice was strained and he remained perfectly still mere inches from her.

"I promise, no regrets," she replied.

She assumed her words would spur him into immediate action, but instead he turned on his side to face her and reached out to stroke a strand of hair away from her face.

"I wasn't expecting this," he said in a soft whisper. "I wasn't expecting you. But that first day when I walked into your home and got my first glimpse of you and saw that saucy sparkle in your eyes, I should have known that you were going to be trouble." His hand lingered on her face, caressing her cheek with a tenderness that only increased her desire for him.

"This has been some crazy ride, hasn't it?" she said, not surprised to find her voice slightly breathless at his touch.

"And it's not over yet." He leaned forward and claimed her lips with his.

His mouth tasted of heat and hunger, and as he touched the tip of his tongue to her lower lip she opened her mouth to allow the kiss to deepen.

He pulled her into his arms and gasped slightly, obviously surprised to find her almost naked in his arms. His skin was hot, almost fevered against her own as the kiss continued growing more hot and more wild with each passing minute.

As he embraced her and she felt the solidness of his chest and of his arms around her, she felt safe for the first time in a very long time.

There were so many things about being held by a man that she'd forgotten—the weight of warm hands on her skin, the tactile pleasure of his chest hair against her bare breasts and the faint rasp of his whiskers as he dragged his mouth slowly down her throat.

His hands stroked her back, as if fascinated by the feel of her skin, as his heart beat a rapid cadence against her own.

She trembled with pleasure as he shifted positions and his hand found one of her breasts. His cupped the fullness and then drew his fingers together to capture her nipple.

He raised his head and gazed down at her, the fire in his eyes igniting an answering heat in her. "You're beautiful," he said, his voice husky.

She wanted to protest, to tell him that she knew she wasn't beautiful, but with his gaze so hot, so hungry on her, she felt more than beautiful.

Once again he claimed her lips with his and his craving for her was evident in the fiery, nearly out-of-control kiss. She gasped against his mouth, her desire rocketing higher than she could ever remember.

She slid her hands down his back, the play of his muscles exciting her. She'd only been with Joe. Her husband had been her first and only lover, and there was something wild and hot about being with a new lover—about being with Riley.

His hand left her breast, and as his mouth slid down her throat to capture her nipple, she tangled her hands in his hair. His tongue teased and raked over the sensitive tip, and sweet sensations rushed through her with each flick of his tongue. Moaning with pleasure, she moved her hips beneath him, wanting more of him, needing all of him.

He didn't hesitate. He swept his hand down the flat of her stomach and then stopped as he encountered her panties.

"Take them off for me." It was an urgent request she couldn't refuse. As she reached down to take them off, he rolled away from her and took off his own briefs.

When they came together again his erection pressed against her thigh as his hand once again slid down the flat of her stomach.

But he didn't caress her where she wanted most, where her need had her half mindless with desire. Instead his hand slid down her hip to her inner thigh.

Over and over again he came precariously close to touching her intimately only to stop short. Arching her hips each time, she thought he might be trying to drive her mad. The promise of ultimate pleasure denied with each caress he gave.

"Touch me," she finally moaned, unable to stand it another minute.

He laughed, the sound both joyous and more than a little bit wicked. "Oh, trust me, Lana. I'm going to touch you. I want to brand you. I want to ruin you for any other man who might come after me."

His words merely stoked her desire higher as a shiver of anticipation shuddered through her. Two could play at his game, she thought. She moved her hand down his stomach, a slow trail of heat, and she felt his muscles clench as she got closer to his hardness.

But instead of touching him there, she slid her hand down his hip. He laughed again, the rumble of his amusement as much a turn-on as anything.

His laughter died on his lips and instead became a low groan when she finally grasped him. He pulsed in her palm and she slowly moved her hand up and then down.

"Okay, you win," he said, the words a guttural groan.

She smiled at him through the haze of her desire. "Maybe I want to ruin you for any woman who comes after me."

"Maybe you already have," he replied, and then he touched her and just that quickly her orgasm crashed in on her. She cried out as she rode the waves of pleasure, and before she was finished he grabbed his wallet from the nightstand, pulled a condom package from it and tore it open.

He had it on in a second and moved over the top of her. She opened her legs to welcome him, wanting more of him.

He eased into her and closed his eyes, as if overwhelmed by her, by them together. He opened his eyes then, and in their green depths she saw not only raw, hot desire but also a vulnerability that threatened to steal the last of her breath away.

Then he moved, drawing back slightly and then plunging deep within her. She closed her eyes and grasped his butt, pulling him farther in, loving the way he filled her up.

His mouth found hers again in a desperate, frantic kiss as his hips rocked against hers with a masterful intensity.

Faster and faster they moved together until she could no longer think, could only feel Riley, inside her and around her.

Once again a tidal wave of sensation approached her and she cried out his name as it overtook her. She was vaguely aware of him stiffening against her as she shattered into a million pieces.

Afterward he rolled to his back and drew a deep breath. "That was amazing," he finally said.

"Yes." It was all she could utter as she waited for

her heart to resume a more normal beat, as she waited for full breath to return to her.

It couldn't possibly have been as amazing for him as it had been for her. She'd always thought Joe was a good lover, but he hadn't even been in the same league as Riley. She now realized Joe had been a selfish lover, taking what he wanted with little thought to her needs. It was painful to admit that had been the story of their marriage.

"I'll be right back." Riley got up from the bed and padded into the bathroom.

She stared after him, exhausted and sated in a way she hadn't been before in her life.

Don't fall in love with him, a little voice whispered inside her head.

He had heartache written in his genes, she knew. Eventually his bodyguard duty with her would be over and he'd be gone. She'd be a fool to allow her heart to get involved with him.

Thank God he'd had protection. She hadn't even thought about it until he had pulled the condom out of his wallet. And of course he kept one in his wallet. A man like Riley would never know when an opportunity might present itself. And she was certain that for a man like Riley, it presented itself often.

He came out of the bathroom and turned out the nightstand lamp, then slid into bed and pulled her into his arms.

"I will guard your slamming-hot body with my life," he said.

She smiled in the darkness of the room. "You're just saying that now because you've had your way with me."

"And what a way it was," he said and planted a soft kiss on her forehead.

Despite her desire not to become emotionally involved with him, she couldn't help the way her heart swelled in her chest.

He stroked her hair and released a deep sigh. "The day I found my mother dead on the floor in our kitchen was the day I made a conscious decision that I was never going to care about anyone again. You got in under my defenses, Lana. You and Haley made me care again."

It was easy to talk about caring for a naked woman you held in your arms after making love to her, she thought. "You shouldn't have made that decision when you did," she replied. "It's like the killer not only murdered your mother, but also murdered you. You have to have the capacity to care. That's what makes us human."

"Yeah, I guess you're right," he replied, but something in his tone of voice made her believe she hadn't responded to him in the way he'd wanted.

"Good night, Riley," she said.

"Good night, Lana," he replied, but didn't loosen his hold on her.

Snuggled against him, she had the feeling she was safe from any danger the world might hold. But she knew it was an illusion. There was only so much a man could do against an unknown assailant.

And if that wasn't enough to worry about, she had to hang on to her heart where Riley Kincaid was concerned. She'd given her heart to Joe and had tried to be all that he wanted, all that he needed. But she'd never been enough. There had always been other women, and with each of Joe's promises to be faithful, she'd eventually lost her love for him. If he hadn't died they would have been divorced.

Riley was far too much like the man she had married, the man who had destroyed her vision of a fairy tale ending. She absolutely, positively refused to make the same mistake twice.

Chapter Ten

Riley looked at his watch and breathed a sigh of relief. Two more hours and they could pack up for good and head home.

The day before had been a nightmare. It seemed as if everyone in the Kansas City area had decided to spend their Saturday at the jewelry show. By the time the day had ended Riley had been beyond exhausted and Lana had been euphoric about the number of sales she'd made.

He now stood next to her, keeping vigil as she showed a necklace to an older woman. He'd thought that after making love to her Friday night she would be out of his system. It had always worked that way for him. He wanted a woman until he had her, and then the hunger was gone.

With Lana it was different. Making love to her had only whetted his appetite and made him hungry for more.

They had made love again last night, and it had

been as wonderful as the first time. Even now as he watched her smile at her customer, as he noticed the way her blond hair fell in a soft wave against her cheek, he wanted her again.

But she'd been unusually quiet this morning as they'd shared breakfast, and he wondered if regrets were already forming in her heart.

She made the sale and then Riley followed her to the pair of chairs and sat. "It's been a lot slower today than it was yesterday," he said.

She nodded. "Sundays are always slow days."

"Have you always designed jewelry?"

"No. I graduated from college with a business degree and then didn't know for sure what I wanted to do with it. I got a job in a jewelry store and it was there that I found my passion. It was also where I was working when I met Joe."

She stared off into the distance, as if her mind was taking her back in time. "The first thing Joe wanted me to do when we got married was quit working. That's when I really began to get serious about making jewelry and designing a line of my own."

"So he was supportive of you."

She turned and looked at Riley and there was a hint of wry amusement in her eyes. "Joe wouldn't have cared if I made paper airplanes as long as it was something I could do at home. Joe supported me in anything that fit into the world he wanted. He liked the idea of a stay-at-home wife, you know, the little lady who could have his meals ready when he got home from work, the one who made sure his uniform was pressed just right and the house was clean."

"That's pretty rare in this day and age," Riley replied.

"So you aren't the kind of man who would like a woman at home whose sole job is caring for your every need?" she asked.

He grinned. "In theory it's every man's fantasy, isn't it? But in reality I would want my wife to be whatever fulfilled her as a person. Making paper airplanes or jewelry or flying a plane—whatever made her happy and successful in her own right."

Once again she looked away from him, but not before he saw the shadow of grief darkening her eyes. He was surprised to realize it depressed him just a little. How long could a woman grieve for a dead man? How long before she would be emotionally ready to go on with her life?

Lana needed a man to love and Haley needed a father, but over and over again she sent him signals that she wasn't ready to move on.

Of course, who was he to question the duration of her grief? He was thirty-three years old and still grieved the loss of his mother when he'd been fifteen years old.

He knew more than anyone that the ability to move on couldn't be forced. He'd had plenty of women over the years who would have loved to force him into caring, into love, but he hadn't been ready or willing—until now. And now that he'd found a woman he wanted, that somehow he thought he might need, she wasn't in a position to accept what he might have to offer her.

He fought back a heavy sigh, wondering how he'd transformed from a selfish bastard who didn't care about anyone to a lovesick man who was probably destined to get his heart broken.

Drawing a deep breath, he froze as he saw a familiar face in the crowd of people. Seth Black was headed their way, a friendly smile not quite reaching his dark eyes.

As Lana stood to greet the potential customer, Riley also got up and smoothly stepped in front of her. "Seth, right?" he said as the big man stepped up to the booth.

"That's right, and you're Riley. Greg told me his neighbor was selling jewelry down here this weekend and I'm always looking for something special for my wife. In fact, our anniversary is coming up, so I thought I'd stop in here and see if I could find something for her."

Lana started to step around Riley, but he held her back. There was no way he wanted her anywhere near this man who was a friend of Greg's. "This is my wife, Lana. She's the creative force, but if you want to buy something, I'm the business end of the operation," Riley said. "Seth was one of the men I played basketball with at Greg's," he told Lana.

"Oh, that's nice." She smiled at Seth, but at the same time placed a hand on Riley's back, as if to assure him that she understood his caution.

Frank Morrel stepped up to the table near Seth, appearing to look over the items, but Riley saw the tension in his fellow agent, a tension that had him ready to spring should Seth try anything stupid.

"Is there something I can show you?" Riley asked Seth. He didn't like the fact that the man had shown up here. Why drive all the way downtown for a piece of jewelry when there were jewelry stores on every corner?

"Maybe a necklace, something pink or red."

Riley showed him several of the necklaces displayed while Lana remained safely behind him. Seth looked at several pieces, made some small talk but ultimately bought nothing.

"Is it just my imagination or was that odd?" Lana asked as he walked away. Frank also wandered away from the table and disappeared from Riley's sight.

Riley stared after Seth and then searched the display tables to make sure he'd left nothing behind— like a sprig of baby's breath. "It was rather strange," he agreed, relieved that the tables bore nothing but Lana's wares. "But the worst thing we could do is make too big a deal of it. We don't know that he's guilty of anything except having a creep for a friend."

He looked at his watch, just wanting this day to be over. He couldn't wait to get Lana back to her own house, where it would be easier to assure her safety.

He clenched his hands into fists at his side. She should have been safe in her own home, but he hadn't forgotten that she'd been attacked there. He hadn't forgotten that if he hadn't walked through the front door when he had she would have been another murder statistic.

He wouldn't let that happen again. For as long as the killer walked free, he didn't intend to leave Lana alone in her home again.

"We can go ahead and start packing up," she said, as if sensing his desire to call an end to the day.

"You've still got a little over an hour left," he protested.

"I'm ready to call it a day and go get Haley." She began to pack up the jewelry that hadn't sold.

"I'll help you in just a minute. I want to make a quick call to Frank Morrel. I want him to meet us at your place and give me an update of the investigation."

With the call made it took nearly half an hour to get everything packed up and back in his car. As they began the drive back to Kerry's house to pick up Haley, Riley once again felt a distance from Lana.

She was quiet and kept her gaze focused out her side window, and he wished he knew what she was thinking, but was afraid of intruding by asking.

"Regrets?" he finally asked, when he could stand her silence no longer.

She turned and looked at him, her expression unreadable. "No," she said after only a moment of hesitation. "No regrets, but when we get back home it's over. I can't have you in my bed anymore."

Somehow he wasn't surprised by her decision. What did surprise him was how much he didn't like her decision. He was well aware that he'd crossed the line in becoming personally involved with her, but he didn't want it to end.

When they reached Kerry's house, Haley exploded out the front door. "Mommy! Daddy! I missed you," she exclaimed as they got out of the car.

Seeing her smiling little face only increased the depression that was slowly settling around Riley's shoulders.

It took only minutes for Lana to thank Kerry and for Riley to get Haley loaded in the car. Haley entertained on the drive back to Lana's, telling them everything she did with her friend Kim. "We played house. I just love Kim," she exclaimed.

Playing house, that's what he'd been doing with Lana, and his game of make-believe had the same results—he'd fallen in love.

Funny, before this particular operation began Riley

had believed he didn't have a heart. He now feared that when he walked away from this, from Lana, he was going to have a broken one.

Agent Frank Morrel was waiting for them when they pulled up in the driveway. He didn't look like an FBI agent, dressed in his casual clothes and leaning on his sports car. Rather, he appeared to be a friend dropping by for a Sunday visit.

At some point in the last few minutes of the drive home Haley had fallen asleep. Lana got out of the car and moved to the back door to get the sleeping child.

"You go on inside. I'll get her," Riley said.

He unbuckled Haley from the seat and gently picked her up. Haley wound her arms around his neck and buried her head in his shoulder as if she belonged there, and Lana felt a wisp of unwanted heat in her stomach as she saw the two of them together.

They greeted Frank and together they all went into the house, where Frank sat at the kitchen table while Lana made coffee and Riley put Haley down in her bed.

As Riley came back into the kitchen Lana felt the sudden need to escape. The weekend had not only been exhausting on a physical level, but she felt as if she'd had too much Riley.

She imagined that his scent still lingered on her skin, that her skin still felt his intimate touches. His laughter filled her head, and she desperately needed to distance herself from him.

"I'm just going to let you two men talk. While Haley is sleeping I think I'll go to my room and rest for a little while," she said.

Immediately Riley's face filled with concern. "Are you all right?"

His obvious concern for her weighed as heavy in her heart as the memory of their lovemaking. "I'm fine," she assured him. "Just tired."

She left them and headed down the hallway to her bedroom. When she reached her room she went directly to the bed and stretched out on her back. Her mind replayed the weekend in excruciating detail.

Fear, drama and exquisite pleasure. The past three days had contained them all. Her mind was having difficulty processing not only everything that had happened but also how she felt about it. How she felt about him.

She had to face the fact. She was falling in love with Riley Kincaid. She didn't want to love him and she definitely didn't want to need him.

She sensed that in the couple of weeks he'd been in her life he'd somehow transformed, become a different man than he'd been when he'd swept through the door on that very first day.

The changes she saw in him frightened her. He'd become softer, more open. She remembered how he'd told her that he'd stopped caring about everyone after his mother's murder but had started caring again with her and Haley. That admission had terrified her.

She didn't want to fall victim to him. She didn't want to believe what she saw shining in his eyes, what she'd felt in his kiss, in his touch.

Once upon a time she'd believed in happily-ever-after with a man like Riley and it had been the biggest mistake of her life. She'd be a complete fool to make the same mistake again.

She rolled over on her side and squeezed her eyes closed, and within minutes she had fallen asleep. She awakened to the scent of his wonderfully spicy cologne and the touch of his hand against her cheek.

"Lana, it's almost eight-thirty. I thought you might want to get up and get some dinner," he said softly.

"Almost eight-thirty?" She shot to a sitting position. "Where's Haley?"

"Back in bed. I fed her and got her into her pajamas and she went right back to sleep," he replied. "I've got a sandwich and chips ready for you." He backed away from the bed. "I'll meet you in the kitchen."

When he left the room Lana swung her legs over the edge of the bed and gave herself a minute to fully awaken. She must have been more exhausted than she'd realized. She'd slept deep and hard.

He'd taken care of Haley while she'd slept. He'd fixed her a sandwich and taken care of things for her. These weren't the kinds of things a bodyguard did. These were the kinds of things a man did for somebody he cared about.

Stop overthinking everything, she commanded herself as she went into the bathroom to wash the sleep from her face. He'd probably just made an extra sandwich when he'd made his own. And as far as taking care of Haley, it might have just been easier for him to deal with it than wake her up.

She left the bathroom and went into the kitchen, where a plate with her dinner sat on the table and Riley stood at the window staring out into the deepening night.

"I can't believe I slept the evening away," she said as she sat.

He turned from the window and offered her a smile. "It's exhausting being an entrepreneur."

"I guess." She picked up the ham-and-cheese sandwich and took a bite as he joined her at the table. "What did you find out from Frank?"

"Seth Black owns a car-repair business. He's married and has no children. He also has no alibi for either the attack on you and at least two of the murders."

"Any history of violence?" she asked. "Any bedwetting, animal abuse or fire starting in his background?" He looked at her in surprise and she smiled. "I watch those crime shows on television, and they always talk about the fact that those things are precursors for serial killers."

"There's nothing specific in Seth's background that we could discern that might indicate he's our man."

"So, you're back to square one." She set her sandwich down as she realized she really wasn't that hungry.

"Not necessarily. I really believe that it's possible that either Trent or Seth is the partner we've been looking for. As we speak, I'm sure their lives are being dissected by every agent available."

"Greg and his partner are overdue for a kill," she said. Even after all that had happened it felt strange to say such a thing, strange to even think such a thing. "The baby's breath that was left on my table was their reminder to me that I'm still the intended victim."

"I refuse to let that happen," Riley exclaimed. He reached across the table and grabbed her hand in his. His eyes radiated with a fierce intensity. "Nobody is going to hurt you again while I'm on duty."

"You won't be on duty forever. Eventually the FBI is going to pull you out of here," she replied and extricated her hand from his.

"That doesn't have to happen. They can tell me the assignment is over, but that doesn't mean I have to leave. I'll stay here as long as you need me, Lana, as long as you want me."

She stared at him. There was something in his tone of voice that made her think he wasn't talking about his job as her bodyguard. She didn't want anything personal from him. After the weekend they'd shared she felt far too vulnerable.

Leaning back in her chair she averted her gaze from his. "I'm sure you're as eager as I am to get this matter resolved so we can both get on with our own lives."

The air felt pregnant with thick emotion as she waited for his reply.

"I'm not eager to get back to my own life."

His words hung in the air and she lifted her gaze to meet his once again. Instead of the ferocity that had marked his expression when he'd talked about protecting her, there was that inviting softness that urged her to melt into him.

He leaned back in the chair and his gaze went out the window where the darkness of night had fallen. "You know, it's funny, for the last eighteen years whenever I thought of my mother, I could only focus on the last time I saw her, dead on the kitchen floor. Somehow it became the only memory I could summon. But in the last couple of days I've been thinking about her a lot and I realize I've got some wonderful memories of her."

Lana remained silent, unsure where the conversation was going. She relaxed slightly as she recognized that he was in the midst of pleasant memories. When he looked at her again a small smile curved his lips and his eyes were the inviting green of lush grass.

"My mother loved to bake," he continued. "Cookies and cakes, pies and tarts. Whenever she had a day off she'd spend it baking. She gave cookies to neighbors, took cakes and pies to the church. On those days when Mom was home and I came home from school, I'd walk in and the whole house would smell. It smelled like home. And that's the way I feel when I walk into this house, Lana. It feels like home."

He'd blindsided her. She hadn't seen where he was going with his story, nor was she quick enough to avoid the physical contact when he reached across the table to take her hand. His words thundered in her head.

"Riley, please," she said, unsure what she was asking of him as she tried to pull her hand from his. But he refused to let go, and fear suddenly increased the rhythm of her heartbeat. It wasn't the kind of fear that Greg inspired, but rather the fear that somehow, someway he'd make her love him more than she already did.

"Lana, I'm in love with you."

"No, you aren't," she protested. "That wasn't part of the deal. I'm just supposed to be another one of your hook-ups." She finally managed to pull her hand free from his. "It was a wonderful weekend, Riley, but that's all it was, a single weekend."

"I want more, Lana. I want a thousand weekends. I'm ready for a lifetime of weekends with you." His eyes shimmered with emotion.

She wanted to yell with joy and weep with sadness at the same time. She had to admit to herself that she was falling in love with him, but she wouldn't repeat her past mistake. She refused to ever consider a relationship with Riley.

"Riley, I told you I wasn't ready for a new man in my life," she said softly as she tamped down her irrational desire to throw herself into his arms.

"Lana, I know you care about me and I know you loved your husband. But Joe is gone and I'm here. Let me in, Lana. I'm a good man. I can be good for you and Haley."

Be strong, she told herself even though she felt as if her heart was breaking. *You have to be strong. Don't let history repeat itself.*

"Of course I care about you. You've been a big part of my life lately. But this isn't real life, Riley, and I imagine once you get back to your real life you'll realize that what you're feeling is pretend love generated by our pretend marriage."

"This isn't pretend for me, Lana," he protested.

She scooted back from the table, needing to get away from him before she did something stupid, before she made the mistake of believing him—and in him.

"I'm sorry, Riley. It has just been pretend for me." She got up from her chair. "I think I'm going to go back to bed. I'm still really exhausted."

Tears burned behind her eyes and a rising emotion filled her chest. "Good night, Riley. And I'm sorry."

He nodded and shifted his gaze to the window, and his shoulders slumped forward slightly. Her last vision of him before she left the kitchen was of a slightly broken man.

Once she was back in her room she threw herself on the bed and buried her face in her pillow, fighting against the deep sobs that threatened to erupt.

This mock marriage with her bodyguard had become far too real for both of them, although in Riley's case she had a feeling love unrequited wouldn't cause too much of a heartache.

Surely there would be plenty of women standing in line eager to console him. A month from now, if he was gone from her house, then she was certain she'd be gone from his mind.

Unfortunately, she knew instinctively that it wouldn't be so easy for her to dismiss him from her mind. He'd reminded her of everything she'd once dreamed of, everything she'd ever hoped for in a marriage. He'd fit perfectly into the mold of her ideal mate, a man who desired and cared about her and loved Haley as well.

She loved the sound of his laughter and that sparkle of humor that so often lit his beautiful eyes. She loved that sometimes when he gazed at her a delicious shiver worked through her.

She could love him like she'd never loved a man

before if she'd allow herself. But she couldn't allow that to happen.

In the beginning she'd loved Joe with all her heart, but by the time of his murder she thought she might have hated him more than a little bit. Joe had insisted he loved her, but he'd had one affair after another and each time promised that it would never happen again.

She feared that any long-term relationship with Riley offered the same kind of ending. She couldn't— she wouldn't—put herself through that twice in a lifetime.

Chapter Eleven

"Daddy Riley, it's time for our tea party," Haley announced. She was clad in a pink princess costume complete with hot-pink plastic heels and a glittering crown on top of her tousled blond curls.

In the two days since he'd confessed his love to Lana, he'd done his best to distance himself not only from her but from the little girl who had also captured his heart. He'd tried to get her to stop calling him Daddy and instead call him Riley and she'd finally compromised by renaming him Daddy Riley.

It was just after seven in the evening as he followed her down the hallway to her bedroom where she'd arranged her little table and chairs in the center of her room.

It had been a gray, cloudy day with heavy clouds threatening rain. About an hour ago a thunderstorm had rumbled through, and when Haley got frightened, Lana had told her to plan a tea party.

The house smelled of baking chocolate. Lana's

contribution to the tea party was homemade cupcakes with rich chocolate icing.

"Teddy is already here," Haley said, and pointed to the big stuffed bear sitting in one of the chairs. "You sit next to him and I'll go get Mommy."

She disappeared out of the room as Riley folded himself up to sit in the small chair. The last two days had been an aching form of agony for him. He and Lana had steered clear of each other. He'd spent most of his time in the living room trying to be as unobtrusive as possible as she went about her daily routine.

At night he lay in the guest room and fought against the depression that threatened to consume him. A broken heart—that's what he had, and he knew the only things that would help it were time and distance from the woman he loved.

His coworkers were beginning to believe that Greg and his partner were now just playing with them, pretending that Lana might be the next victim while they set their sights on somebody else.

Riley wasn't willing to take a chance on them being wrong. He was determined to stay here until Greg and his partner were behind bars or until he went insane with wanting Lana.

He forced a smile as she came into the room with Haley. "Mommy, sit there," Haley instructed and pointed to the seat across from Riley.

Lana offered him a distant smile and sat in the

chair. She looked beautiful in a pair of denim shorts and a turquoise blouse that did amazing things to her eyes. "Isn't this nice?" she said with a forced cheerfulness. "I was just thinking yesterday that I was in the mood for a tea party."

"Yeah, me, too," Riley agreed in an effort to get with the program. "And I'm so glad Teddy could make it. I know his days are busy getting honey."

Haley giggled. "Teddy loves honey, but he loves tea parties more," she said in a very grown-up voice. "And now I'll pour the tea."

She made a big show of picking up the plastic teapot and pouring them each make-believe tea. Riley lifted his little cup to his lips and slurped loudly. "That's the best tea I've ever tasted," he said as he lowered the cup.

As Haley giggled once again he caught Lana's gaze, and for a moment there was such warmth in those blue depths he could scarcely draw another breath.

She quickly averted her gaze from his and lifted her cup to her lips, those lips that he wanted desperately to kiss until they spoke the words of love he wanted to hear.

For the next few minutes Haley entertained them as they drank pretend tea and ate the freshly baked chocolate cupcakes. She kept the conversation flowing by chatting about anything and everything that entered her mind and by translating whatever Teddy had to say.

Riley tried desperately to stay focused on Haley, but his gaze and his every thought kept returning to the woman seated across from him.

She looked tired and stressed-out, and he could only guess that his little confession of love had somehow added to her burden. That wasn't what he'd wanted. In his head he'd had a vision of an entirely different outcome.

Maybe he was the fool. Maybe he really was the arrogant, conceited ass she'd initially pegged him as when he'd first arrived in her home.

He'd been in her house less than a month and he'd expected her to love him more than the late husband she'd been married to for five years. He'd expected her to love him more than any other man she might ever meet for the rest of her life.

He suddenly realized both Lana and Haley were looking at him expectantly. What had he missed? "Excuse me?"

"I said I want to ask you a very important question, Daddy Riley. You have to pay attention," Haley exclaimed as she placed her hands on her hips.

He bit his lower lip to hide his smile of amusement as his heart swelled with love for the tiny tot. "I'm sorry. I'm paying attention now. What's your question?"

She sidled up next to him and looped a little arm

around his shoulder. "I wanted to ask you when I could have a baby sister or brother."

Riley shot a startled look to Lana, who looked equally surprised by her daughter's question. Haley looked at him, obviously impatient for an answer. "Oh, honey, I really think that's up to your mother," he said, throwing the ball directly into Lana's court.

"Not for a long time," Lana replied. "Maybe after you start school."

Thankfully, that answer seemed to satisfy Haley.

A little while later the party was called due to bath and bedtime. As Lana attended to her daughter, Riley went back into the living room and stood at the back windows, staring out without seeing.

He'd faced a hundred dangerous situations over the course of his career and he'd survived them all, but he wasn't sure how long he would be able to survive remaining in this house with Lana.

It was torture, loving her and knowing that she didn't return his feelings. He didn't know how to make her love him. He felt as if he'd given her what he had to give and it hadn't been enough.

He would have already made arrangements for another agent to take over his duty but he hated the idea of any other man seeing Lana with her hair sleep-tousled as she came into the kitchen for her first cup of hot tea. He hated to think of another man laughing with her when darkness fell outside and the house felt cozy and intimate.

But he also realized that each and every day he stayed would only make it more difficult on Haley when he left. As much as he hated to see Lana cry, he definitely couldn't stand the thought of Haley's tears.

Dammit, he wanted to be the father in Haley's life. He wanted to be the man to hold her when she cried, to teach her about life and laugh with her. He wanted to be the man who walked her to the bus on the first day of school, the man who would walk her down the aisle on the day she got married.

Even worse, he wanted to be the man who woke up every morning with Lana in his bed. He didn't just want to protect her from all the bad guys in the world, he wanted to be the good guy in her life.

He'd been a player all his life, but he didn't want to play anymore. He wanted a real life with a family he adored and the same woman by his side until the very end.

He turned away from the window as Lana came into the living room. The very sight of her ached deep in his heart. "She asleep?" he asked.

She nodded. "Out like a light. I'm going to get a glass of wine. Would you like one?"

"Sure, why not?"

"Why don't you just sit and relax and I'll bring it

out here," she said, as if she didn't want him following her into the kitchen.

He agreed and flopped down on the sofa, his heartache once again weighing heavy in his chest. She returned a moment later with a glass of wine in each hand. She handed him one and then sat with her own in the chair opposite the sofa.

The tension that had become almost unbearable during the last two days seemed to grow tauter as they sipped their wine in silence.

Finally he could stand it no longer. "Lana, I didn't want me telling you how I felt about you to create more problems in your life," he said as he set his wineglass on the coffee table.

Her gaze lingered on his face, and her features gave him all kinds of mixed messages. Her eyes were soft and filled with what he thought was want and yearning, and yet her lips were compressed tightly together as if in rejection.

With a sigh she worried one hand through her hair, mussing it just enough to look charming. "Riley, I still think once you get back to your own life you're going to realize that you just got caught up in a game of pretend." She offered him a smile that didn't quite reach the depths of her eyes. "You'll get back to your hook-ups and hot dates and won't even think about me."

"That's not true." He leaned forward and picked up his wineglass once again. "If nothing else comes from this, Lana, I've realized that I'm ready to be a husband, that I want to be a father. I'd hoped it would be with you and Haley."

He couldn't keep the wistfulness out of his voice. Pride be damned, he wanted her to know that the man who'd walked into her house weeks ago was not the same man who would be walking out.

"It was easy to be content with uncommitted relationships when my heart wasn't involved," he continued. He fell silent and took another sip of his wine, his gaze lingering on her as she stared past him and out the window.

"Lana, I'm going to tell you this one more time. I love you, and I love Haley, and there's nothing I'd rather do than be the man in your lives."

When she met his gaze her eyes were filled with a yearning that made him believe that she loved him, too, that she wanted him in her life forever. But she shook her head. "I'm sorry, Riley. It's just not meant to be."

He hadn't really expected anything different, but her words formed a hard, painful lump in the center of his chest. "Then maybe it would be best if I contact Larry and tell him that he needs to assign another agent to you."

For a moment he thought she was going to protest. For one joyous second he saw love shining from her eyes and he believed it was all going to be okay.

But that emotion quickly doused and she raised

her shoulders in a small shrug. "You do whatever you think best, Riley."

What would be best was if at the end of all this they wound up together. What would be best was if she'd confess that she cared about him as deeply, as passionately as he did her.

He frowned thoughtfully as he considered pulling himself off the case. There were other things to consider besides his own emotional state.

"If another agent comes in, then Greg will know something is up," he said.

"What difference does it make?" she countered. "At this point in the game he knows I've been attacked. He also knows that perhaps the police told me about the relevance of the baby's breath. I really don't care what he thinks or knows about what's going on in my house. I just want all this over and done."

There was a weariness in her tone that let him know she was reaching the end of her rope. She tipped the last of her wine into her mouth and then stood. She wore her mental exhaustion in the slight sag of her shoulders, in the tight line of her lips.

"I'm going to call it a night. You can tell me what your plans are in the morning." She carried her wine-glass into the kitchen and placed it in the dishwasher, then returned to the living room.

"Good night, Riley," she said, then headed down the hallway toward her bedroom. Riley watched her go, his heart in his throat.

Stay or go? He needed to make a decision. The best thing for Lana's world was for him to stay, for them to continue their fake relationship until something broke with the investigation.

His head told him to stay, but his heart urged him to go before it got so painful he never recovered. With a weariness of his own he grabbed his empty wineglass and pulled himself up off the sofa at the same time that Lana screamed from the bedroom.

He dropped the glass as he roared down the hallway, his heart thundering with the burst of adrenaline that sizzled through him.

She met him in the hall, her eyes wide with terror. "A man," she gasped. "He was wearing a ski mask and was breaking in through the bedroom window."

It was obvious to him that she was okay, so he turned on his heels and raced for the front door. As he hit the front porch he saw a figure in the distance running up the street.

He took off after the intruder, determined that this time the man wasn't going to get away. He was vaguely aware of footsteps behind him as he raced down the sidewalk. Turning his head, but not breaking his speed, he saw Frank struggling to catch up.

The dark sky lit up with a flash of lightning followed by a deep rumble of thunder, but the turbulence of Mother Nature had nothing on the wild emotions crashing through Riley.

Within minutes his lungs burned and his legs

ached, but he didn't slow and began to steadily gain on the figure in the distance while Frank fell further behind.

It wasn't Greg. The person was slighter in build than Lana's neighbor. Trent or Seth? It was impossible to tell who it was with the ski mask that covered his hair. Trent or Seth or somebody else who hadn't even made it onto their radar?

There was no question that this man was Greg's partner, the man they'd all been looking to find. It was far too great a coincidence that Lana had been marked as the next victim and this man had been caught trying to break into her house.

"Halt," he yelled after they'd gone almost four blocks. He pulled his gun from his holster as he continued to race forward. "Stop or I'll shoot you in the back and ask questions later!"

The figure stumbled, as if in hesitation, and then slowed, obviously believing Riley's threat. He came to a halt and slowly turned to face Riley, his long arms held up in the air.

With the ski mask and the dark shadows of night, Riley still couldn't identify the culprit even as he drew close enough to hear his labored breathing.

"Lie face down," Riley instructed. "With your arms out at your sides."

"Just don't shoot me," the man said as he followed Riley's instructions.

Riley frowned. He didn't sound like Seth or Trent, but his voice was definitely familiar.

As Riley patted him down to look for weapons, Frank rushed up to help. "Who is it?" he asked.

"I'll know in a minute," Riley replied. "He's clean." He stepped back. "Sit up," he commanded.

What Riley wanted to do was beat the hell out of the man on the ground for making Lana scream, for all the lives he'd destroyed.

"Get that ski mask off," Riley said. Frank had his gun drawn and leveled at the man as well. The creep definitely wasn't going anywhere. "And if you twitch wrong it will be the last move you ever make."

He reached up and pulled off the ski mask at the same time a flash of lightning rent the sky. Riley fought back a gasp of surprise.

Randy Newsom, Greg's nephew.

"Jeez, I don't know what everyone is so excited about. I was just after some cash," he exclaimed. "I wasn't going to hurt anyone."

"Get up," Frank said and pulled a pair of handcuffs from his back pocket.

"Ah, come on, can't you just let me go?" Randy asked. "Look, I'm sorry," he said to Riley. His brown eyes glittered darkly. "It was a dumb move on my part. I just thought you might have some cash lying around in the bedroom."

"Get up and turn around," Frank repeated.

"Can't we talk about this?" Randy asked as he

slowly rose to his feet, a pleading expression on his face. "My mom is going to be so upset, and her boyfriend is going to bust me up."

"You should have thought about that before now," Frank said as he cuffed the kid.

Riley's head was spinning, working overtime to make sense of this newest development. Randy had attempted this latest break-in. Was he also responsible for the initial attack on Lana?

"Besides, you don't have to worry about what your mother's old man is going to do to you," Frank said. "You're looking at the death penalty."

"For what? Last I heard breaking and entering doesn't get you the death penalty," Randy replied.

"Yeah, but conspiracy in four murders does," Frank replied.

Randy offered Frank a sly smile as another flash of lightning lit the sky. "You can't prove that. You can't prove anything except I was committing a robbery. I'm a juvenile, an honor student who's never been in trouble. I'll be out of jail before you two get back to wherever you came from."

The teenager's smugness bothered Riley. He was missing something…something important. Thunder boomed overhead.

Why would Randy break into the house knowing Riley was there, knowing that it was possible he'd be caught? It didn't make sense. It was almost as if he'd wanted to be caught. Was it part of a plan to draw

Riley away from the house? So that his partner could do the dirty work? And just who was his partner?

His brother, Ricky?

While he and Frank were here dealing with Randy, where was Ricky?

Jesus, was it possible that Greg didn't have one partner, but two? The horrible thought roared through his brain. Two malleable teenagers who could be manipulated to kill?

Randy had run straight down the sidewalk when he could have darted into the darkness of somebody's backyard and disappeared. He'd made it relatively easy for Riley to catch him. Why?

To waste time. To draw Riley out of the house, leaving Lana alone and vulnerable.

Lana!

Fear ripped through his gut, a frantic fear like he'd never felt before. "Take care of this and get somebody at Greg's house to arrest him," Riley said to Frank as he tore down the sidewalk in the direction of the house, praying that he wasn't too late.

Lana stood in Haley's doorway, grateful her scream hadn't awakened the child. Lana usually joked that nothing short of an atomic explosion could wake up Haley once she'd fallen asleep. Tonight she was grateful for that fact.

With her arms wrapped around herself to ward off

the chill that threatened to consume her, she walked to the front door and peered outside.

The only sound was the occasional rumble of thunder. She had no idea in what direction Riley had run when he'd taken off. Surely this time he'd get the man who'd tried to break in. Hopefully, this was the beginning of the end of this whole mess.

She closed and locked the front door, afraid to keep it unlocked while she was in the house alone. The chill she'd tried to avoid snaked up her back and formed a ball of ice in the pit of her stomach.

Hot tea. That's what she needed. As she headed for the kitchen she tried not to think about Riley and what might be happening outside.

Riley had a gun. Surely he would be safe. Surely she would have heard a gunshot if there had been any real trouble.

Her hands trembled as she pulled a cup from the cabinet, and when she turned to get a tea bag from the pantry, he stepped out.

The cup she held crashed to the floor as she saw the man in the ski mask facing her. A horrible sense of déjà vu filled her as her mind worked to make sense of it. Had he somehow managed to lose Riley and doubled back here?

He moved to a position between her and the doorway into the living room, blocking her from leaving the kitchen. He looked smaller than she remembered, thinner and not quite as tall. But the knife he held was as wicked-looking as she remembered from the last encounter.

"What do you want?" she cried. "Why are you doing this?" Desperately she looked around for something she could grab, a weapon of some sort that she could use to protect herself, but there was nothing.

He pulled a sprig of baby's breath from his pocket and set it on the countertop. "For the innocent," he said. "We're saving kids from being beaten and abused by stepfathers."

Riley, where are you?

The back door. Maybe she could escape through the back door. *Keep him talking,* a little voice whispered in her head. *Buy as much time as you can.*

"But why are you killing the women?" she asked, and took a sliding step toward the door. "Why not kill the abusive men?"

"Because it's a mother's job to protect her children," he cried, and his voice broke in the middle of the sentence.

At that moment Lana realized who stood before her, his eyes glittering wildly behind the mask as he wielded the evil-looking knife.

"Ricky," she said in shock. "Ricky, listen to me. Riley isn't my husband. We aren't married. He's an FBI agent who moved in here to watch your uncle." The words tumbled out of her as she slid another step closer to the back door. "I don't fit your profile,

Ricky. I haven't brought a stepfather into Haley's life."

He froze for a moment and tilted his head as if in confusion. "Shut up," he said, and snapped rigid. "I don't want to hear your lies."

Drawing a deep breath, Lana released a sob and sprang for the back door. There was a roar in her ears as she fumbled with the doorknob, but the roar silenced as he stabbed her in the back of her shoulder.

She reeled backward, the excruciating pain stealing her breath, and he sliced her arm. As he came toward her again she kicked him and managed to get the table between them. She could feel the blood pouring both from her arm and down her back, felt a nauseating weakness begin to take over as the pain pulsed through her.

"Ricky, please," she sobbed. "Please stop this now."

"I can't. He told us that you were next. It's my mission." Ricky shoved the table aside as if it were a stick of firewood.

"It's not a mission. It's murder," she cried.

She wanted to yell, desperately wanted to scream, but she was afraid, so afraid that Haley might stumble onto the scene.

Even though Riley had told her that so far they had never hurt a child, she couldn't take the chance that Haley might be their first.

"It's my duty," he hissed as he surged forward to attack her once again. Instinctively she raised her leg to kick him. She missed.

Blood smeared across the top of the table as she stumbled against it. She felt weak, and with each second that passed she was getting more light-headed.

Summoning all the strength she had left, she kicked him once again, this time connecting solidly to his midsection. As he stumbled backward she ran in the only direction she could, toward the laundry room and pantry.

She was almost to the door when he tackled her from behind. The pain in her back once again threatened to consume her, but she rolled over and kicked at him as she scrabbled across the floor on her back like a frightened crab.

Tears blurred her vision, and she'd never felt so cold in her life. And tired. She was so very tired. But her will to live was too great to give up.

Ricky roared with anger as he moved in, the knife held high overhead. With a whimper, Lana managed to scoot into the laundry room. She slammed the door and leaned heavily against it as he banged on it from the other side.

Seated on the floor, she used all her weight to keep him from pushing open the door, but she knew it was only a matter of minutes before her weakness overwhelmed her, before the darkness that flirted at the edge of her consciousness swept in.

She began to quietly sob as visions of Haley filled her brain. Haley, who loved everyone and everything that life had to offer. Haley, who loved tea parties and teddy bears and her mommy—and Riley.

Riley. A picture of his strong, handsome face exploded in her head. Had she been a fool to turn away from his love? It didn't matter now. Nothing mattered.

As she felt the door crack open an inch and heard Ricky's grunts of exertion, the darkness that had threatened stole in and she knew no more.

Chapter Twelve

Lana.

Her name echoed in Riley's head as he ran down the sidewalk toward her house. His heart felt as if it was going to explode out of his chest. His stress level was so high he felt as if he might vomit.

Randy and Ricky.

They'd flown under the radar because of their youth, because they'd never been in trouble before and were honor students. Dammit, they hadn't even been on the suspect list as far as Riley knew.

Lightning ripped apart the sky followed by a low rumble of thunder. He felt the storm in his veins, and a wild cacophony of screaming emotion filled his head with a jumble of thoughts.

Not Lana, he pleaded. *For God's sake don't let him hurt her.* Haley would be lost without her mother, and somehow Riley felt as if he'd be completely lost if Lana were no longer on this earth.

It didn't matter that she didn't want to be with him. He didn't care that she obviously didn't love him as deeply as he did her. The very fact that he did love her had given him a kind of hope for himself and for his future that had been lacking in the past.

He thought it might be raining, but he realized the mist in his vision was tears. Tears of rage and of an icy fear he'd never felt before.

When he reached the house he was grateful to see a patrol car pulling up in Greg's driveway. Good, at least he didn't have to worry about Greg getting in his way.

He raced to Lana's front door and tried to get in, but the door was locked. He fought back a scream of impotent rage, aware that every second counted.

With a trembling hand he yanked his set of keys from his pocket and stabbed the appropriate one into the lock. With a strangled gasp, he unlocked the door and shoved inside, his gun held tight in his hand.

Silence.

It was the kind of silence that raised the hairs on the nape of his neck, the kind of tomblike silence that created a cold wash of fear over him.

"Lana?" He called her name softly as he moved from the entryway to the living room.

There was no reply. He paused at the mouth of the hallway, unsure in which direction to go. He knew she wouldn't have gone back to bed after Randy tried to break in that window. The fact that she hadn't been standing at the front door waiting for Riley to return twisted his gut.

Something was wrong.

The silence was too profound.

"Lana?" he called again, and moved cautiously down the hallway. He came to the bathroom first and whirled inside, his gun clutched in both his hands, ready to defend himself as he searched for Lana.

Nothing.

He next came to Haley's room, and as he saw the little girl sleeping soundly on her back, her little chest rising and falling with each deep breath, he nearly fell to his knees in relief.

But where was Lana?

The guest room and her master suite were also empty, with no signs of a struggle, no sign that anything dire had occurred.

He walked back down the hallway silently, his pulse pounding in his head as he walked through the living room toward the kitchen.

The lingering scent of baked cupcakes hung in the air and set off a crazy sense of déjà vu for him. His stomach clenched and his feet suddenly felt as if they weighed a million pounds.

He saw the blood first, smeared across the kitchen table and across the floor. The sight of it froze him in his tracks.

Just like before.

It was history repeating itself. The gun nearly slipped from his sweaty hand as he took a step forward. More blood on the floor.

He was fifteen years old once again and looking for his mother. He stared at the kitchen island before him, afraid to look on the other side, afraid of what he might find there on the floor.

But it wouldn't be his mother. His mother had been gone for years. Lana. If it was Lana's blood then she had been hurt. He had to find her, and he prayed that for a second time in his life he wasn't too late.

He tightened his grip on his gun and saw that the back door was open. Had Ricky somehow managed to drag Lana out of the house?

Drawing a deep breath, he stepped around the island, a whoosh of relief escaping him as he saw nobody crumpled on the floor.

He whirled around as he heard somebody behind him.

Agent Bill McDonald froze as Riley leveled his gun at him.

"You nearly got shot," Riley said as he lowered the gun. "Ricky Newsom. He was here, but he must have run out the back door."

"Frank radioed it in. Greg and Randy are in custody, and we have agents already looking for Ricky."

Bill looked around, his features taut with tension. "Have you found Lana?"

Riley shook his head, a hollow emptiness filling his chest. He followed Bill's gaze and noticed the smear of blood that appeared to lead to the laundry room.

The closed door called to him, whispering in tones that were a combination of hope and horror. He exchanged a quick glance with Bill and on wooden legs moved to the door.

He turned the knob and pushed, but something kept the door from opening more than an inch. But in that inch he saw a splash of sandy-blond hair and his heart seemed to stop as he realized it was the weight of her body keeping the door from opening.

"Lana," he screamed her name at the same time he was aware of Bill calling for an ambulance. Using as much caution as possible he pushed again on the door, horrified to realize she was either dead or unconscious as her body slowly moved with the weight of the door.

Blood.

It was everywhere in the small room. Too much blood, he thought. Deep sobs swelled up inside him as he finally managed to get the door open wide enough for him to slide inside.

Instantly he crouched down next to her, just as one

of the sobs he'd held in so tightly escaped from him. He felt a weak, reedy pulse in her wrist.

"She's alive," he yelled to Bill. "Lana, stay with me," he said as he held tightly to her hand. He was afraid to move her, afraid that he might cause the bleeding to get worse.

She was on her back and he could see the slice on her arm but couldn't tell where else she'd been hurt. The wound on her arm didn't appear to be serious enough to have caused all the blood loss. He didn't see any other wounds on her but feared what might be on her back.

He continued to hold her cold hand and talk to her as he waited for the ambulance to arrive. It seemed to take an eternity, but finally the emergency responders arrived and moved Riley out of the way.

As they worked to load her on a gurney, a loud clap of thunder shook the house and he heard a faint cry from Haley's bedroom.

Knowing there was nothing more he could do for the woman he loved, he elbowed his way through the FBI agents who had arrived on the scene and ran down the hallway.

Haley met him in the doorway, her eyes as big as saucers. "Thunder!" she exclaimed in the same tone she would use to say "monster." "I want my mommy."

Riley lifted her up in his arms. "Mommy is sick

right now and some nice men are going to take her to the hospital."

"Will she be all right?" Haley tightened her arms around his neck.

Riley hesitated. At this moment in time he had no idea if Lana was going to be okay or not. He didn't want to lie to Haley, yet he didn't want to frighten her anymore than she already was.

"We hope she's going to be fine," he finally replied. He fought against the swelling emotion in his chest.

"Who is going to take care of me?" Haley asked in a little voice.

"Daddy Riley is," he replied and hugged the little girl closer against his chest.

She laid her head on his shoulder and relaxed. "I love you, Daddy Riley," she said against the crook of his neck.

It took all the willpower he had not to break down into tears. "I love you, too," he whispered hoarsely.

Now all they could do was wait to see if the woman they both loved had managed to survive the vicious attack.

Lana awoke in the early morning. The sun was just rising outside her hospital-room window. The back of her shoulder ached and her bandaged arm stung, but they were good hurts, the kind that let her know she had survived the night of terror.

Her first real thought was of Haley, but oddly enough the thought brought with it no real concern. There was no doubt in her mind that Riley was taking care of her daughter.

Funny that she trusted him completely with the most precious thing in her life and yet wouldn't trust him with her heart.

She felt fuzzy and suspected that the IV drip she was hooked to contained some kind of pain medicine. The events of the night seemed very far away.

She closed her eyes and must have fallen asleep again, because when she next awakened the sun was full up and Riley was sitting in a chair next to her bed.

He was asleep, and she remained still and allowed herself to drink in his features. She loved the length of his dark eyelashes and the straight line of his nose. She loved the strength in his features and the soft, gentle curve of his lips.

She loved him. She loved him more than she'd ever loved her husband, more than she'd ever believed possible. And that love frightened her.

His eyes opened and she found herself staring into those gorgeous evergreen-colored depths. For a moment he said nothing but instead released a sigh she instantly recognized as relief.

She punched the button to raise the head of her bed. "I guess I'm going to survive?"

He smiled and scooted his chair closer to the bed. He looked tired. Lines of stress cut deep across his forehead, and his dark hair looked as if he'd raked his hands through it a hundred times. "You took a little mending and a blood transfusion, but the doctors have all assured me you will have a swift and complete recovery."

His smile crumpled. "I can't believe how close I came to losing you." His voice trembled with his emotion. "When I walked into that kitchen and saw all that blood, knew that you'd been hurt, I nearly died."

Lana's heart crunched as she saw the depth of his emotion. She didn't want to acknowledge it. It hurt to even think about it.

"Haley?" she asked.

"I dropped her off at Kerry's about an hour ago. She told me to tell you that she loves you and you make better French toast than I do."

Lana smiled, but the smile lasted only a moment as she thought of the night before. "You know it was Ricky Newsom."

Riley nodded. "He was picked up two blocks from your house still wearing the ski mask and with enough of your blood on him to assure his arrest. Randy and Greg have also been arrested. Ricky and

Randy are saying that the murders were all Greg's idea and Greg is maintaining that he had nothing to do with any of it."

Lana looked at him worriedly. "Does that mean there's a chance that Greg will be freed?"

"Not a chance in hell," he assured her. "It seems your neighborhood serial killer liked to keep little mementos from his kills—a hair barrette, a half-eaten granola bar and several other odd things from the victims. Ricky told our agents where Greg kept those things in his house, and it's only a matter of time before the lab confirms that those items belonged to the victims. We've got him, Lana. We've got them all."

"Thank God," she replied. "But isn't it odd, that three men would be working together to murder so many women?"

"Extremely odd," he agreed. "From what Ricky has been telling our men, Greg was badly abused by a man who came into his mother's life when he was young. The two boys also have the same kind of problem with the man their mother moved into the house. Greg managed to manipulate and tap into their anger."

He hesitated, and she could see there was more. "What? What else?"

"They think he killed your husband, Lana. They believe that there were two murders a couple of years ago and that it's possible Joe had gotten suspicious and Greg thought him to be a threat. I'm sorry, Lana. I know how much you loved your husband." Riley's eyes held a wealth of sympathy. "He must have been one hell of a man to keep you bound to him even after his death."

She sighed wearily. It didn't seem fair for her to send Riley away without him knowing the truth. "I did love Joe…in the beginning, but by the time of his murder I was preparing to divorce him."

Riley looked at her in surprise. "What? But why?"

She gazed at him and then looked down at the pale white sheet that covered her. "You remind me of him, Riley. He was handsome as sin and the kind of man who couldn't help himself from flirting. It came to him as naturally as breathing."

She paused a moment as old, painful memories rushed in, memories she'd tried for almost two years to forget. "We'd been married a little over a year when he had the first affair."

She looked up at Riley, glad she didn't see pity shining from his eyes. That's the last thing she wanted from him, had been the last thing she'd ever wanted from anyone.

"That first time, he said all the right things. It had been a slip, he was sorry, and more than any-thing he wanted me and our marriage to work." She gave a mirthless laugh. "And being the fool I was, I believed him. He cheated again while I was in the hospital having Haley, and again he made all kinds of promises and I forgave him."

She felt stupid that she'd clung onto Joe for as long as she had despite his lies and cheating. She'd been so naive to believe him each and every time he'd cried and begged her to give him another chance.

"I wanted to make the marriage work, but by the time of his death I knew it was time for me to move on. He was a weak man and he thought I was a weak woman who would continue to overlook his infidelity. He'd ruined my hopes, destroyed any dream I might have had for a happy future with him. By the time of his murder I was ready to walk away from him."

"And nobody knew about these affairs? You never told your sister or any of your friends?" He leaned forward, close enough now that she could smell him, that scent that would always remind her of tender passion and warm safety.

"Everyone loved Joe, and I didn't want to ruin his reputation. I just figured when the time came I'd tell everyone we'd grown apart. And then he was dead and I didn't tell anyone anything."

She sighed. "And as much as I was sorry that he'd been killed and that Haley had lost her father, I was ready to move on."

He leaned back in his chair and studied her

features, his own impossible for her to read. "So it isn't grief that's keeping you from loving me. You just really don't love me."

Her heart ached more than whatever Ricky had done to her back as she saw the wealth of pain in his eyes. "That's not true. I do love you, but I'm not willing to put myself through the same thing twice. Riley, you're just like Joe—bigger than life and a shameless flirt."

Emotion pressed hard in her chest, causing tears to form in her eyes. "I can't do it again, Riley. I won't put myself through it again."

"I'm not asking you to," he replied. Once again he leaned forward, and this time he reached for her hand and took it into his. His fingers enveloped hers with warmth and strength. "You've forgotten one very important difference between Joe and me. He was a married man, and any flirting I've done in my life I've done as a single man."

He squeezed her hand. "I'm not Joe, Lana. Don't let your experience with him destroy any chance of happiness we could find together. Let me be the man who gives you back your hopes, who gives you back your dreams. I love you, Lana, and there's no other woman I want in my life. Give me a chance. Give us a chance."

She saw his love shining from his amazing green

eyes, felt it in the warmth of his hand, and a crazy hope built up inside her.

Maybe she was wrong to expect from him the same hurtful results that had occurred with Joe.

She'd told Riley that after his mother's murder it had been tragic that he'd closed himself off to caring for anyone. But wasn't she doing the same thing now?

"You scare me, Riley Kincaid," she said softly.

He smiled, that wonderfully sexy smile that caused her heart to beat just a little bit faster. "No more than you scare me. Lana, I've been looking for you for most of my life. Now that I found you I don't intend to let you go easily."

"You've definitely caught me at a weak moment," she said.

His eyes darkened and filled with a sense of horror as his fingers tightened around hers. "We almost lost you. When I think of what might have happened if you hadn't been able to get into the laundry room it makes me sick."

"But I did manage to get into the laundry room, and I'm here now."

"I'm warning you, Lana. When you get well and you're out of that hospital bed, I intend to sweep you completely off your feet."

"I'd like that," she replied and realized it was true. "I think I'm ready to be swept off my feet by you."

The fire that leaped into his eyes warmed her from head to toe and she believed in him, believed in them, and as he leaned over and gently kissed her cheek, she believed that this time she was going to get her happily-ever-after.

Epilogue

"Daddy Riley is here!" Haley called from the front window.

Lana's heart jumped in anticipation, despite the fact that she'd just seen him the night before. She gave a final glance to the Christmas tree as she hurried to the front door to let him inside.

"Ho, ho, ho!" he said as he stepped into the entry hall, his arms laden with wrapped packages as he was chased in by the cold December air.

"Daddy Riley, you sound just like Santa Claus," Haley exclaimed.

"I feel like Santa with all these presents," he replied as he offered Lana one of those smiles that made her feel hot and bothered and wonderfully alive.

"Are some of those presents maybe for me?" Haley asked.

Riley laughed. "Maybe." He walked into the living room and unloaded his arms, then took off his leather coat and grabbed Lana around the waist. "And how are you?"

"I'm wonderful. We have hot cocoa and cookies ready in the kitchen. Haley knows she has to go to bed early so that Santa can come while she's asleep."

"I'm almost sleepy now," Haley exclaimed.

"Then we'd better have our cocoa and cookies," Riley said as he released Lana.

Minutes later they all sat around the kitchen table enjoying cookies shaped like Christmas trees and cocoa loaded with marshmallows.

As Riley spun a story for Haley about Santa's trip across the world, Lana's heart swelled with happiness. It had been almost six months since that horrible night when Ricky had attacked her, and in those six months she had given her heart and soul to Riley.

Although technically he still lived in his downtown apartment, at least four times a week he ended up spending the night here with Lana and Haley.

Greg, Ricky and Randy were all in jail awaiting trial. Both Ricky and Randy were being tried as adults, and the district attorney was confident that all three of them would never get out of prison.

It was almost nine when Lana joined Riley on the sofa. Haley was asleep with dreams of presents when the morning came and Lana and Riley had hauled out all the gifts that they'd had hidden in the guest-room closet for days.

She snuggled against him and released a contented sigh. Later they would go to bed and he'd make sweet love to her, but for now she was content to cuddle in his arms as the tree lights twinkled and lit the room with a romantic glow.

"This is the first Christmas in a very long time that I feel truly at peace with myself and the world," he said as he caressed her hair.

"I feel exactly the same way," she replied. "And it's all because of you."

He smiled. "I was going to say the very same thing. Lana, I've loved what we've been doing for the last six months, but it's not enough." He straightened and pulled a small ring box from his pocket.

Instantly her heart began to beat a faster rhythm. Somehow she'd known this moment was coming. He'd been wonderfully patient with her need to take things slow, but the last couple of weeks she'd sensed an impatience in him.

"Marry me, Lana. Put me out of my misery and marry me."

In the past six months she'd learned what kind of a man Riley was. A strong, honorable man who was definitely devoted to Haley and her.

Before she answered him she searched her heart to find any doubt, any hesitation, but there was none. All that was in her heart was a shining love and complete trust.

"Yes," she said. "Yes, I think it's about time we make our pretend marriage real."

His eyes gleamed as he opened the box to reveal a beautiful diamond ring. He removed it and slid it onto her finger. "You know what this means. You now have a bodyguard for life."

"Thank God it doesn't look like I'm going to need a bodyguard in my life anymore," she replied as her heart sang with happiness. "But I do need you, Riley. I want you to be the man who raises Haley. I want you to be the man who is beside me for the rest of my life."

Joe had broken her heart and made it hard for her to trust again, but Riley had taught her not only to trust again but also to believe in her dreams of a happy ending.

As he leaned over and kissed her, his lips held not only the taste of passion, but also the kind of love Lana knew would last a lifetime.

* * * * *

HARLEQUIN®

A Romance

FOR EVERY MOOD™

Spotlight on

── Heart & Home ──

Heartwarming romances
where love can happen
right when you least expect it.

See the next page to enjoy a sneak peek
from Harlequin Superromance®,
a Heart and Home series.

Enjoy a sneak peek at fan favorite Molly O'Keefe's
Harlequin Superromance miniseries,
THE NOTORIOUS O'NEILLS, *with*
TYLER O'NEILL'S REDEMPTION,
available September 2010
only from Harlequin Superromance.

Police chief Juliette Tremblant recognized the shape of the man strolling down the street—in as calm and leisurely fashion as if it were the middle of the day rather than midnight. She slowed her car, convinced her eyes were playing tricks on her. It had been a long time since Tyler O'Neill had been seen in this town.

As she pulled to a stop at the curb, he turned toward her, and her heart about stopped.

"What the hell are you doing here, Tyler?"

"Well, if it isn't Juliette Tremblant." He made his way over to her, then leaned down so he could look her in the eye. He was close enough to touch.

Juliette was not, repeat, *not* going to touch Tyler O'Neill. Not with her fingers. Not with a ten-foot pole. There would be no touching. Which was too bad, since it was the only way she was ever going to convince herself the man standing in front of her—as rumpled and heart-stoppingly handsome now as he'd been at sixteen—was real.

And not a figment of all her furious revenge dreams.

"What are you doing back in Bonne Terre?" she asked.

"The manor is sitting empty," Tyler said and shrugged, as though his arriving out of the blue after ten years was casual. "Seems like someone should be watching over the family home."

"You?" She laughed at the very notion of him being here for any unselfish reason. "Please."

He stared at her for a second, then smiled. Her heart fluttered against her chest—a small mechanical bird powered by that smile.

"You're right." But that cryptic comment was all he offered.

Juliette bit her lip against the other questions.

Why did you go?

Why didn't you write? Call?

What did I do?

But what would be the point? Ten years of silence were all the answer she really needed.

She had sworn off feeling anything for this man long ago. Yet one look at him and all the old hurt and rage resurfaced as though they'd been waiting for the chance. That made her mad.

She put the car in gear, determined not to waste another minute thinking about Tyler O'Neill. "Have a good night, Tyler," she said, liking all the cool "go screw yourself" she managed to fit into those words.

It seems Juliette has an old score to settle with Tyler.
Pick up TYLER O'NEILL'S REDEMPTION
to see how he makes it up to her.
Available September 2010,
only from Harlequin Superromance.

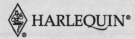

HARLEQUIN®

TANYA MICHAELS
Texas Baby

Instant parenthood is turning Addie Caine's life upside down. Caring for her young nephew and infant niece is rewarding—but exhausting! So when a gorgeous man named Giff Baker starts a short-term assignment at her office, Addie knows there's no time for romance. Yet Giff seems to be in hot pursuit.... Is this part of his job, or can he really be falling for her? And her chaotic, ready-made family!

**Available September 2010
wherever books are sold.**

"LOVE, HOME & HAPPINESS"

HARLEQUIN
Ambassadors

Want to share your passion for reading Harlequin® Books?

Become a Harlequin Ambassador!

Harlequin Ambassadors are a group of passionate and well-connected readers who are willing to share their joy of reading Harlequin® books with family and friends.

You'll be sent all the tools you need to spark great conversation, including free books!

All we ask is that you share the romance with your friends and family!

You'll also be invited to have a say in new book ideas and exchange opinions with women just like you!

To see if you qualify* to be a Harlequin Ambassador, please visit www.HarlequinAmbassadors.com.

*Please note that not everyone who applies to be a Harlequin Ambassador will qualify. For more information please visit www.HarlequinAmbassadors.com.

Thank you for your participation.

BAP09BPA